Romantic Comedy

FORMS OF DRAMA

Forms of Drama meets the need for accessible, mid-length volumes that offer undergraduate readers authoritative guides to the distinct forms of global drama. From classical Greek tragedy to Chinese pear garden theatre, cabaret to kathakali, the series equips readers with models and methodologies for analysing a wide range of performance practices and engaging with these as 'craft'.

SERIES EDITOR: SIMON SHEPHERD

Romantic Comedy

Trevor R. Griffiths

methuen | drama

LONDON • NEW YORK • OXFORD • NEW DELHI • SYDNEY

METHUEN DRAMA
Bloomsbury Publishing Plc
50 Bedford Square, London, WC1B 3DP, UK
1385 Broadway, New York, NY 10018, USA
29 Earlsfort Terrace, Dublin 2, Ireland

BLOOMSBURY, METHUEN DRAMA and the Methuen Drama logo
are trademarks of Bloomsbury Publishing Plc

First published in Great Britain 2022
This paperback edition published 2023

Series design by Charlotte Daniels

A catalogue record for this book is available from the British Library.

Library of Congress Cataloging-in-Publication Data
Names: Griffiths, Trevor R., author.
Title: Romantic comedy / Trevor R. Griffiths.
Description: London ; New York : Methuen Drama, 2022. | Series: Forms of
drama | Includes bibliographical references and index. |
Identifiers: LCCN 2021038911 (print) | LCCN 2021038912 (ebook) | ISBN
9781350183377 (hardback) | ISBN 9781350183414 (paperback) | ISBN
9781350183391 (ebook) | ISBN 9781350183384 (epub)
Subjects: LCSH: Love in literature. | English drama–History and criticism. |
Comedy–History and criticism. | Comic, The, in literature. | LCGFT: Literary criticism.
Classification: LCC PR635.L68 G75 2022 (print) | LCC PR635.L68 (ebook) |
DDC 822/.0523093543–dc23/eng/20211115
LC record available at https://lccn.loc.gov/2021038911
LC ebook record available at https://lccn.loc.gov/2021038912

ISBN: HB: 978-1-3501-8337-7
            PB: 978-1-3501-8341-4
            ePDF: 978-1-3501-8339-1
            eBook: 978-1-3501-8338-4

Series: Forms of Drama

Typeset by Integra Software Services Pvt. Ltd.

To find out more about our authors and books visit www.bloomsbury.com and sign up
for our newsletters.

To my children,
David and Sara,
and to their children,
Zac, Gabriella, Amelie and Joseph.

CONTENTS

LIST OF ILLUSTRATIONS

SERIES PREFACE

The scope of this series is scripted aesthetic activity that works by means of personation.

Scripting is done in a wide variety of ways. It may, most obviously, be the more or less detailed written text familiar in the stage play of the western tradition, which not only provides lines to be spoken but directions for speaking them. Or it may be a set of instructions, a structure or scenario, on the basis of which performers improvise, drawing, as they do so, on an already learnt repertoire of routines and responses. Or there may be nothing written, just sets of rules, arrangements and even speeches orally handed down over time. The effectiveness of such unwritten scripting can be seen in the behaviour of audiences, who, without reading a script, have learnt how to conduct themselves appropriately at the different activities they attend. For one of the key things that unwritten script specifies and assumes is the relationship between the various groups of participants, including the separation, or not, between doers and watchers.

What is scripted is specifically an aesthetic activity. That specification distinguishes drama from non-aesthetic activity using personation. Following the work of Erving Goffman in the mid-1950s, especially his book *The Presentation of Self in Everyday Life*, the social sciences have made us richly aware of the various ways in which human interactions are performed. Going shopping, for example, is a performance in that we present a version of ourselves in each encounter we make. We may indeed have changed our clothes before setting out. This, though, is a social performance.

The distinction between social performance and aesthetic activity is not clear-cut. The two sorts of practice overlap

xiv   SERIES PREFACE

and mingle with one another. An activity may be more or less aesthetic, but the crucial distinguishing feature is the status of the aesthetic element. Going shopping may contain an aesthetic element – decisions about clothes and shoes to wear – but its purpose is not deliberately to make an aesthetic activity or to mark itself as different from everyday social life. The aesthetic element is not regarded as a general requirement. By contrast a court-room trial may be seen as a social performance, in that it has an important social function, but it is at the same time extensively scripted, with prepared speeches, costumes and choreography. This scripted aesthetic element assists the social function in that it conveys a sense of more than everyday importance and authority to proceedings which can have life-changing impact. Unlike the activity of going shopping the aesthetic element here is not optional. Derived from tradition it is a required component that gives the specific identity to the activity.

It is defined as an activity in that, in a way different from a painting of Rembrandt's mother or a statue of Ramesses II, something is made to happen over time. And, unlike a symphony concert or firework display, that activity works by means of personation. Such personation may be done by imitating and interpreting – 'inhabiting' – other human beings, fictional or historical, and it may use the bodies of human performers or puppets. But it may also be done by a performer who produces a version of their own self, such as a stand-up comedian or court official on duty, or by a performer who, through doing the event, acquires a self with special status as with the *hijras* securing their sacredness by doing the ritual practice of *badhai*.

Some people prefer to call many of these sorts of scripted aesthetic events not drama but cultural performance. But there are problems with this. First, such labelling tends to keep in place an old-fashioned idea of western scholarship that drama, with its origins in ancient Greece, is a specifically European 'high' art. Everything outside it is then potentially, and damagingly, consigned to a domain which may be neither 'art' nor 'high'. Instead the European stage play and its like can best be regarded as a subset of the general category, distinct from the rest in that two groups of people come together in order specifically to present and watch a story being acted out by imitating other persons and settings. Thus the performance of a stage play in this tradition consists of two levels of activity using personation: the interaction of audience and performers and the interaction between characters in a fictional story.

The second problem with the category of cultural performance is that it downplays the significance and persistence of script, in all its varieties. With its roots in the traditional behaviours and beliefs of a society script gives specific instructions for the form – the materials, the structure and sequence – of the aesthetic activity, the drama. So too, as we have noted, script defines the relationships between those who are present in different capacities at the event.

It is only by attending to what is scripted, to the form of the drama, that we can best analyze its functions and pleasures. At its most simple analysis of form enables us to distinguish between different sorts of aesthetic activity. The masks used in *kathakali* look different from those used in *commedia dell'arte*. They are made of different materials, designs and colours. The roots of those differences lie in their separate cultural traditions and systems of living. For similar reasons the puppets of *karagoz* and *wayang* differ. But perhaps more importantly the attention to form provides a basis for exploring the operation and effects of a particular work. Those who regularly participate in and watch drama, of whatever sort, learn to recognize and remember the forms of what they see and hear. When one drama has family resemblances to another, in its organization and use of materials, structure and sequences, those who attend it develop expectations as to how it will – or indeed should – operate. It then becomes possible to specify how a particular work subverts, challenges or enhances these expectations.

Expectation doesn't only govern response to individual works, however. It can shape, indeed has shaped, assumptions about which dramas are worth studying. It is well established that Asia has ancient and rich dramatic traditions, from the Indian sub-continent to Japan, as does Europe, and these are studied with enthusiasm. But there is much less wide-spread activity, at least in western universities, in relation to the traditions of, say, Africa, Latin America and the Middle East. Secondly, even within the recognized traditions, there are assumptions that some dramas are more 'artistic', or indeed more 'serious', 'higher' even, than others. Thus it may be assumed that *noh* or classical tragedy will require the sort of close attention to craft which is not necessary for mumming or *badhai*.

Both sets of assumptions here keep in place a system which allocates value. This series aims to counteract a discriminatory value system by ranging as widely as possible across world practices and by giving the same sort of attention to all the forms it features. Thus book-length studies of forms such as *al-halqa*, *hana keaka* and *ta'zieh* will appear in English for perhaps the first time. Those studies, just like those of *kathakali*, tragicomedy and the rest, will adopt the same basic approach. That approach consists of an historical overview of the development of a form combined with, indeed anchored in, detailed analysis of examples and case studies. One of the benefits of properly detailed analysis is that it can reveal the construction which gives a work the appearance of being serious, artistic, and indeed 'high'.

What does that work of construction is script. This series is grounded in the idea that all forms of drama have scripts of some kind and that an understanding of drama, of any sort, has to include analysis of that script. In taking this approach books in this series again challenge an assumption which has in recent times governed the study of drama. Deriving from the supposed, but artificial, distinction between cultural performance and drama, many accounts of cultural performance ignore its scriptedness and assume that the proper way of studying it is simply to describe how its practitioners behave and what they make. This is useful enough, but to leave it at that is to produce something that looks like a form of lesser anthropology. The description of behaviours is only the first step in that it establishes what the script is. The next step is to analyze how the script and form work and how they create effect.

But it goes further than this. The close-up analyses of materials, structures and sequences – of scripted forms – show how they emerge from and connect deeply back into the modes of life and belief to which they are necessary. They tell us in short why, in any culture, the drama needs to be done. Thus by adopting this extended model of drama, and by approaching all dramas in the same way, the books in this series aim to tell us why, in all societies, the activities of scripted aesthetic personation – dramas – keep happening, and need to keep happening.

I am grateful, as always, to Mick Wallis for helping me to think through these issues. Any clumsiness or stupidity is entirely my own.

Simon Shepherd

ACKNOWLEDGEMENTS

The research for this book was completed over many years at the University of Warwick, Strathclyde University and the Polytechnic/University of North London/London Metropolitan University. I am grateful for the institutional help and support that enabled me to conduct that research. My gratitude to the supervisors and examiners of my PhD (G. K. Hunter, David Mayer, Arthur Scouten, Stanley Wells and Peter Thomson) and to my colleagues for the benefit of their guidance, counsel, criticism and encouragement cannot easily be expressed. My co-authors and co-editors, Colin Counsell, Margaret Llewellyn-Jones, Kenneth McLeish, Sue Smith and Carole Woddis have further encouraged me in considering many of the complexities involved in the history of Romantic Comedy. I am also grateful to Simon Shepherd, the editor of this series, for many years of constructive debate about key issues in theatre history. He, and they are, of course, not responsible for any opinions, or errors in what I say here, but they have contributed immensely to my thinking about the issue of Romantic Comedy. My research has been conducted in the libraries of institutions including Warwick, Strathclyde and North London as well as at London University, the British Library, the Victoria and Albert Museum, the Folger Shakespeare Library, the New York Public Library, the Harvard Theatre Collection, the Birmingham Shakespeare Library, and the Shakespeare Centre Library in Stratford upon Avon. I am very grateful for the help and support of the staff at those institutions. I enjoyed giving papers related to this topic at Amherst College, the RSC Summer School, the University of Kent and for the Society for Theatre Research.

As well as my academic debts, I would like to express my thanks to all those who helped in other ways, with accommodation, childcare and medical support over the years. To my children, David and Sara, my apologies for sometimes being distracted by comedy, and to my wife, Kathy Rooney, 'thanks,/And thanks, and ever thanks' (Shakespeare [1623] 2008: 3.3.14–15).

Earlier version of parts of my discussions of *The Man of Mode*, *The Country Wife*, *The Way of the World*, *She Stoops to Conquer* and *London Assurance* first appeared in the introductions to my Nick Hern Books editions of these plays. Any material used is with the kind permission of Nick Hern of Nick Hern Books.

The author and publisher gratefully acknowledge the permission granted to reproduce the copyright material in this book. *Private Lives* © Noël Coward, [1930] 2000, *Private Lives*, Methuen Drama, an imprint of Bloomsbury Publishing Plc. *Meet the Mukherjees* © Tanika Gupta, 2008, *Meet the Mukherjees*, Oberon Books, an imprint of Bloomsbury Publishing Plc. *Stags and Hens* © Willy Russell, 1996, *Stags and Hens* in *Russell Plays: 1*, Methuen Drama, an imprint of Bloomsbury Publishing Plc.

Every effort has been made to trace copyright holders and to obtain their permission for the use of copyright material. However, if any have been inadvertently overlooked, the publishers will be pleased, if notified of any omissions, to make the necessary arrangement at the first opportunity.

CONVENTIONS

In the Introduction (pp 1–15) dates are marked as BCE or CE to help differentiate works from different periods. Thereafter, unless noted, all dates are CE.

In citations from Shakespeare act and scene numbers are designated thus: 1.1.

Speech prefixes and stage directions have been silently regularized in quotations from plays.

Newspaper Reviews are quoted from *Theatre Record* with the exception of those for *Hindle Wakes*, which are taken from the British Newspaper Archive.

Introduction:
'The Course of True Love'

Lysander: Ay me! for aught that I could ever read,
 Could ever hear by tale or history,
 The course of true love never did run smooth;
 But either it was different in blood –
Hermia: O cross, too high to be enthralled to low!
Lysander: Or else misgrafted in respect of years –
Hermia: O spite, too old to be engaged to young!
Lysander: Or else it stood upon the choice of friends –
Hermia: O hell, to choose love by another's eyes!
Lysander: Or, if there were a sympathy in choice,
 War, death or sickness did lay siege to it
…
Hermia: If then true lovers have been ever crossed,
 It stands as an edict in destiny.
 Then let us teach our trial patience
 Because it is a customary cross,
 As due to love as thoughts and dreams and sighs,
 Wishes and tears, poor fancy's followers.
    (Shakespeare [1600] 2017: 1.1.132–42, 150–5)

Contexts

In this dialogue from *A Midsummer Night's Dream* William
Shakespeare (1564–1616) presents his audience with an
account of the general characteristics of Romantic Comedy that
accurately delineates the perennial themes and narrative arcs
of a genre that has proved enduringly popular in the Western
tradition from some of the earliest known comedies to the
present. Fathers (and it is instructive that in these patriarchal
societies mothers seldom appear), whatever the particular
configuration of their societies, are presented as concerned
with the disposal of their daughters and sons into marriages
that preserve and, if possible, enhance the value of their estates
(either land or goods) and maintain their status as citizens.
Traditionally, Romantic Comedy has been about a young man
and a young woman overcoming such patriarchal obstacles
to reach a socially sanctioned recognition of the validity of
their love. However, as this study will show, the process of
achieving a settled place in the face of many challenges en
route often casts light on both the fragility of social norms
and the pretensions of the lovers themselves. Traditional
Romantic Comedies demonstrate that there are many ways
of reconciling the apparent contradictions presented in the
opening scenes in outcomes that suggest fruitful resolutions of
initially apparently irreconcilable conflicts.

Romantic Comedy is a form of drama in which the main
impetus of the action is the protagonists' attempts to find
an appropriate sexual partner in the face of either external
opposition (e.g. patriarchal fathers who want their daughters
to marry for social status or money, not love), or internal
contradictions (e.g. lack of self-knowledge leading to an
inability to recognize true feelings) or a mixture of both. The
simple formulation that boy meets girl (or latterly boy meets
boy, girl meets girl etc.), boy loses girl, boy finds girl and
they live happily ever after can generate an infinite number
of complications that make it extraordinarily difficult to pin
down a definition of Romantic Comedy that does not appear

banal on the one hand or over-general on the other. Romantic Comedies may be variously satirical or farcical, comedies of manners or tragicomedy, narrative romances or fairy tales. Many Romantic Comedies rely on elements of Comedy of Manners,[1] while the complications that ensue when there are two pairs of potential romantic lovers can lead to farce or at least farcical moments. The enduring popularity of Romantic Comedy owes much to the near universality of its subject matter and to the opportunities it offers to audiences to share vicariously the triumphs of true love, since in a typical Romantic Comedy there is seldom room to doubt that the concluding marriages provide anything other than a happy ending.

Societies structure themselves in a variety of ways creating often overtly unacknowledged conventions and practices that place their members in specific social, cultural and political positions and offering them ways in which to view the world and make sense of their locations within it. Those positions are often considered by a society as simply natural or 'just how things are', until they come under scrutiny because they disable rather than enhance individuals' choices. As Edmund Leach said in 1973 in a brief formulation that still resonates today:

> Taken together these rules and conventions serve to carve up the social environment into a vast array of cross-cutting classes of things and persons in terms of which we organize our daily lives. ... Any infringement of the standard conventions generates a sense of emotional shock which we experience *either* as embarrassment *or* as excitement.
>
> And even in a story, any reference to a transgression of taboo, however oblique, creates vicarious excitement.
>
> [P]rimary myths are always centrally preoccupied with persons and creatures who are wrongly constructed or wrongly born or in the wrong place, and with such universal moral offences as homicide, sexual misdemeanours and abnormal food behaviour. Such myths exhibit the limits of normality and the potent dangers of otherness by turning normality back to front.
>
> (Leach in Robey 1973: 51–2)

Traditionally Romantic Comedy has been heteronormative, responding to social conventions that delineate heterosexual partnerships as key to the maintenance of patriarchal structures in which the transmission of material goods within a family group through time is seen as a significant element in maintaining social stability. However, romantic love is potentially disruptive and even destructive of the patriarchal order, since it pits the individual's desires against societal norms and its untrammelled power must be curbed if the social order is to be maintained. At the same time, the absurdities of the exercise of patriarchal power must in some way accommodate and give way to the desires and needs of the individual lovers. Lessons learnt on stage are applicable to those being addressed in the auditorium.

In looking at examples of Romantic Comedy drawn from some 2,500 years it is important to recognize that any generalization about actual sexual behaviour in the times and places that provide the original context of the works should probably be hedged about with so many provisos that it would be qualified out of existence. My choice of examples for consideration attempts to give due weight to some important plays and to locate them within their Romantic Comedy contexts, using a main example and a second example in each section in order to facilitate consideration of some key issues in their making or critical reactions to them. I have thought it best to assume no great prior knowledge of some factors that may impinge on how a work was received when it was first staged. This necessitates a degree of contextualization that may sometimes touch on material that may be well known to some of my readers. By necessity this is not a straightforward history of every English Romantic Comedy ever staged. However, it offers a guide to key moments and key works that can illuminate how the genre has tended to operate over the years and to some key issues that the genre has been preoccupied with.[2] In particular, when I consider a selection of works of the last hundred years or so, I have chosen to explore works that challenge what had been the norm in many previous centuries, at the expense of works that may be seen as continuing the Romantic Comedy heritage relatively unchanged.

Drama itself at any point has its own conventions that may determine a particular approach to writing or staging plays, rather than being necessarily concerned with representing accurately a particular aspect of what people may actually do in life outside the theatre. For the ancient Greeks and Romans, for example, the fact that actors were masked was an underpinning element of their theatrical practice; for the Greeks and Romans and the English audiences of the early modern period, the working assumption was that the actors of female parts were male; in contemporary British theatre, on the other hand, there may be fluid casting in which an actor's gender does not necessarily equate with the gender of the character they are playing and, inasmuch as there may be a presumptive assumption or prior history of a role usually being played by an actor of a particular racial type or gender, that too may be challenged. There is, then, in Romantic Comedy a kind of double coding in which the conventions of everyday life outside the theatre may need to be considered alongside a special set of conventions that are specific to theatre itself. It is the exploration and challenging of both sets of conventions that can create the vicarious excitement that Leach postulates as characteristic of our engagement with the breaking of taboo.

Greek and Roman Comedy

The first surviving examples of Romantic Comedy come from ancient Greece and Rome and they influenced subsequent comedies in a variety of ways both directly and indirectly. Attitudes towards sexual activity have changed over time and according to age, class, location and gender. It is clear, for example, that Athenian and Roman examples of Romantic Comedy have quite different attitudes towards pre-marital sex and rape to those that would be most common in current Western society. Athenian law operated on hugely different principles to contemporary British legal assumptions as did Roman law, so that in the Roman plays by authors such as

Plautus (254–184 BCE) and Terence (between 195/185–59 BCE) that were adapted from Greek originals by writers such as Menander (*c*.341/2–290 BCE), we cannot be certain that the plays provide accurate indications of precisely what a particular society actually believed or encoded in its laws and conventions governing sexual behaviour.[3] Nevertheless, there is sufficient information to be able to argue that the key elements of Romantic Comedy as practised by Menander, Plautus and Terence focused on the question of social standing and its importance in ensuring the onward transmission of the right to citizenship and of household assets, a factor that has remained significant throughout the centuries.

The theatrical seeds from which such complex and multifaceted plays as *A Midsummer Night's Dream* (1596 CE) and *Twelfth Night* (1601 CE) grow are to be found in this so-called New Comedy of Menander and the Roman works of Plautus and Terence that were directly inspired by Menander and his contemporaries. Together, they laid down a groundwork in which a young man desires an apparently unobtainable woman and, often with help of a witty servant, slave or companion, frustrates the negative efforts of various patriarchal figures to thwart his plans. Although Menander's plays were effectively lost for many centuries, the Roman plays that were heavily indebted to them were a major influence on Shakespeare's Romantic Comedy and laid down templates that were consciously and unconsciously followed through successive generations, particularly in the Comedies of Manners of the late seventeenth century and such derivatives as Oliver Goldsmith's *She Stoops to Conquer* (1773 CE). However, these Greek and Roman early prototypes lack something that was to become one of the most significant factors in later examples of the genre: the female beloved in Menander, Plautus and Terence is a minor figure, an object of love rather than an active figure in her own narrative. She is effectively powerless to affect her fortunes or her eventual fate through her own agency. The full flowering of Romantic Comedy can only come when the female lover gains her voice.

It is extremely hard to make definitive statements about the origins of Romantic Comedy as a theatrical form. There are many analogues in ancient Greek stories of the exploits of the gods and in folk tales and the prose narratives called romances, where the pursuit of a beloved in the face of obstacles, both natural and supernatural, leads to a pairing of a man and a woman when tasks are completed or quests concluded.[4] The plays of Aristophanes (*c*. 446–386 BCE), the oldest complete comedies that survive from ancient Greece, are both more obviously political and more fantastic than those of Menander and less concerned with romantic love, but recent scholarship has benefitted greatly from the idea that the personal is political and that Menander was concerned with serious political issues that could be explored through domestic milieux and societal concerns. However, if we choose to differentiate between the Old Comedy of Aristophanes and the New Comedy of Menander, we can recognize some significant differences. Although when generalizing from only the extant work, we should always be mindful that what survives is only a tiny proportion of the drama of ancient Greece and Rome, we can say that Menander chose domestic topics rather than the fantastic and mythic stories developed by Aristophanes and that he presents scenarios that are more overtly concerned with the everyday practices and customs of life in contemporary Athens rather than with the high politics that figures so much in Aristophanes's plays: for Menander agriculture and marriage predominate rather than trips to the underworld or to Cloud Cuckoo Land. However we define realism, Menander appears to be offering us relatively realistic pictures of Athenian everyday life in which families engage in farming or drawing water from wells, cooking, and feasting, falling out and reconciling with neighbours. Compared to Aristophanes the shape of the plays has also changed considerably, with the chorus reduced from a major feature of the script with a significant role to play in the action to no more than a stage direction referring to a group of rowdies.[5]

Menander

Menander is the only writer of Greek New Comedy whose work has survived the vicissitudes of time and there are only two (virtually) complete plays currently extant. His reputation in classical times was extremely high and grammarians often cited short extracts from the plays to exemplify good linguistic practice but the most complete of his plays was only discovered in 1952 CE when it emerged in part of the lining of a mummy that was being unwrapped. One of the great paradoxes of Romantic Comedy is that works by Menander, who is effectively the first known writer of recognizable Romantic Comedies, were acknowledged as the source of many plays by the Roman writers Plautus and Terence. However, Menander's works were largely unknown in anything like their complete form for many centuries, so that by the time two more or less complete plays came to light at the end of the nineteenth and in the middle of the twentieth centuries the genre had moved on under the influence of the Roman dramatists whose work began to be staged again from the fifteenth century and was to be found in the school curriculum.

We cannot be sure how true to actual life Menander's plays are and from a modern viewpoint we might wish that we were allowed more access to the inner life of characters, particularly the female beloved who remains a very shadowy construct, often without a voice and even without a name. Nevertheless, these plays do provide us with a starting point from which to trace the beginnings of Romantic Comedy. *Dyskolos* (variously translated as *The Grouch*, *The Misanthrope*, *The Curmudgeon*, *The Bad-tempered Man* or *Old Cantankerous*) and *Samia* (generally known as *The Girl from Samos*) offer two slightly different strands of action but in both cases the plot centres on finding a way of circumventing obstacles placed in the way of a lover by a series of what will become the very familiar difficulties of the genre. In *Dyskolos* the god Pan who speaks the prologue simply declares that the young man Sostratos has fallen in love with Knemon's daughter 'by a touch of magic' (Menander 1994: 128), so that his love is treated simply as a given. Although Sostratos sends go-betweens to negotiate his pursuit of Knemon's daughter, he has never actually met her or spoken to her until she appears on stage to draw water from a spring at the shrine to Pan that occupies the centre of the stage space. The Daughter herself is entirely preoccupied with the consequences of Simiche, her father's servant, having lost a bucket down the well, although she is happy to accept Sostratos's help in fetching water. They do have a further scene together after her father has also fallen down the well, but while Sostratos moons about in a lovestruck fashion they have extraordinarily little interaction by modern standards, and she is mainly concerned with her father's predicament. Eventually Knemon is rescued and has been sufficiently affected by his predicament to appoint his stepson Gorgias as his proxy in deciding about a marriage for the daughter. Gorgias has been on Sostratos' side for some time and is happy to broker the marriage to his stepsister. Since Sostratos is the son of the wealthy Callippides he is able to persuade his father in turn that Gorgias should marry Sostratos's sister thus bringing together the two families' landholdings. Meanwhile Knemon is browbeaten into joining the celebrations at the shrine of Pan. So, the play concludes with two couples betrothed, a communal feast and Knemon's forced integration into the celebration. The germs of future developments are here but so too are factors that would not be fully incorporated into the genre. From a modern perspective we have little to go on in respect of thoughts about the future successes of the marriages, except Pan's declaration in the prologue that he cares about Knemon's daughter's future, which may have cast enough of a penumbra of benevolence over the action for its contemporary audience. Familiar as we now are with four people in a courtship dance in which potential misalliances are ultimately averted, the union of two couples, where one pair have scarcely spoken to one another and one member of the other couple only appears onstage once, is rather disappointingly underdeveloped, but we must remember that the conventions of the period were quite different and that stage action may have added a dimension of interaction, reinforcement or undercutting of the extant lines. Certainly, the idea that the protagonist wants to marry a young woman and is beset by obstacles in the form of physical tasks that must be completed to qualify him for the role and that he must also negotiate obstruction from interested parties is well-established here. Moreover, the pattern of would-be helpers and would-be hinderers suggests the close analogies between this genre and the folk tales, narrative romances and fairy tales that deal with romantic love in non-theatrical forms.

There are significant differences between the plots of the two substantially extant plays of Menander, *Dyskolos* and *Samia*. In *Samia* (315?, 309? BCE) the plot depends on the unravelling of complications caused by coincidences. Demeas and Nikeratos have been away on a long business trip and have agreed that Moschion, the adopted son of Demeas will marry Nikeratos' daughter Plangon. Unknown to them, Moschion has impregnated Plangon, and she has had a baby. Moschion wishes to marry her, but he is afraid of facing his father to ask permission. Chrysis, Demeas's mistress (the woman from Samos of the title), has also had a baby, which has died, although Demeas had anyway given instructions that it should be exposed and left to die, as it was illegitimate. When the fathers return, they discover Chrysis who is nursing Plangon's baby and mayhem ensues as a complicated series of cross-purposes begin. Demeas wants to get rid of Chrysis after he sees her feeding Plangon's baby, because he manages to convince himself that Moschion has had an affair with Chrysis, and that the baby is actually Moschion's. Of course, this is partly untrue since the baby is Plangon's not Chrysis's, although he is right about its paternity. None of those who know the true situation can manage to get the whole story out as confusion proliferates, until eventually Moschion manages to reveal the truth and everyone is reconciled, Plangon and Moschion are married, and the baby is legitimized. Clearly one social assumption is that Plangon is happy to have her baby legitimized and that she is also happy to forgive Moschion for what may well have been him raping her (the extant text is unclear as to whether he raped or seduced her, only revealing that he is embarrassed about the situation that has developed) and another is that the two patriarchs have planned for the union anyway. There are obvious parallels with the stories of Perdita's exposure in *The Winter's Tale* (1612 CE) and the plans of the fathers in *She Stoops to Conquer*, as well as the general atmosphere of mistakes, unvoiced assumptions, coincidences and misunderstandings that characterize much later Romantic Comedy.

In *Dyskolos*, the status of the beloved is in no doubt as far as the protagonist is concerned: she is eligible to marry him because no difficulties as far as legitimacy and social position are involved. The obstacle to a marriage is in the perceived character of her father who has the potential to veto the marriage solely by virtue of him being her father. Only when the action of the play has administered a series of domestic shocks does the father realize that he is far too misanthropic to do his fatherly duty, forcing him to enlist a proxy to deal with the real world on his behalf. Although he is tricked and bullied into joining in a concluding feast, he is not a model citizen and until late in the play, he would prefer to be outside the dramatic closure of the action.

The critic, Northrop Frye, pointed to the expulsion of the scapegoat as a conspicuous characteristic of Aristophanic comedy in which the comic action is designed to result in the purging of an irritant from society to its greater good (1957: 45). Romantic Comedy has also often been aware of the danger that expelling the outsider can itself undercut the comic resolution. The character who is only grudgingly dragged into the concluding harmony, be it a feast or a dance, remains a familiar figure in much later comedy in such figures as Jacques in *As You Like It* (1600 CE) or, in even more extreme forms, Malvolio in *Twelfth Night* and Shylock in *Merchant of Venice* (1597 CE). While *Merchant of Venice* is probably the most extreme example of such an expulsion in a Romantic Comedy, with the defeat of Shylock casting a long shadow over the ultimate comic resolution, Romantic Comedies often try to find a way of at least mitigating the effect of the discomforting of the outsider: in *Twelfth Night*, for example, the extended plotting after the gulling of Malvolio does not entirely threaten the comic synthesis but it can leave a bitter taste, compounded by the play's final words being left to another outsider, Feste, with his rain raining every day. Similarly, in *She Stoops to Conquer*, the disruptive impetus associated with Tony Lumpkin is assimilated by his willing acceptance of his new-found status, but his mother, Mrs Hardcastle, who remains somewhat underwhelmed by events and unreconciled to her defeats, only has access to the comic synthesis through her husband's love. These are important factors to contrasted to the impetus towards reconciliation that often characterizes Romantic Comedy and Stanley Cavell also quotes Frye calling

> particular attention to the special nature of the forgiving and forgetting asked for at the conclusion of romantic comedy: 'Normally, we can forget in this way only when we wake up from a dream, when we pass from one world into another, and we often have to think of the main action of a comedy as "the mistakes of a night," as taking place in a dream or nightmare world that the final scene suddenly removes us from and thereby makes illusory.'
>
> (Cavell 1981: 51)

Plautus and Terence

The Roman dramatists Plautus and Terence are the two writers whose extant works are the only complete examples of a genre named *comoedia palliata* (comedy in Greek dress), which flourished in Rome in the second century BCE. As with Menander, so with Plautus and Terence, the plays operate in simulacrum of an apparently realistic observed everyday life, but our sense of this apparently observational quality must be tempered by an understanding of the complex relationship between the method of the plays' composition and both Roman and Athenian life. The Roman authors generally took their plots directly from Greek originals but chose to combine material from two Greek plays to create their own works (a practice known as 'contaminatio'). While this means that we have some access to the Greek originals through the Latin plays, particularly through contemporary or later commentary, prologues and the like, we do not unfortunately have direct evidence of how any extant complete Roman play maps onto any Greek originals, since there is a mismatch between what survives from Greece and what survives from Rome: none of the extant Latin plays derives directly from any of the extant works by Menander. In some cases we may be able to detect a Greek social model behind a Roman façade but there may well also be a bending of that original both in how the Greek original treated its material and then a further refraction through the medium of the Latin play.[6]

Of the two Roman writers, Plautus contributed directly to the comic tradition through his play *Menaechmi* (also known as *The Brothers Menaechmus* or *The Two Menaechmuses*), which provided the basis of the plot of Shakespeare's *Comedy of Errors* (1592 CE) and, to a lesser extent, his *Twelfth Night*. Both Plautus and Terence were staples of the English grammar school curriculum and there is no serious doubt that Shakespeare would have encountered them in his schooldays, assuming that he was educated at King Edward's School in Stratford.[7] There are also parallels with the scenarios of the Italian *Commedia dell' Arte* and plays within the *Commedia Erudita* tradition. In Plautus's play a twin searching for his long-lost brother finds himself in the town where the lost twin is not only living but has both a wife and a mistress. After much confusion about who the twins really are, the mistakes are ironed out, although there is very little engagement with or sympathy for either wife or mistress who are distinctly subordinated to interest in the twins. Both of Shakespeare's plays rely on mistakes about who twins really are, although he does not use twin servants in *Twelfth Night* and in both his plays the romantic issues are more important than they are in Plautus.

Comparing Terence with Plautus is slightly difficult, since we may ultimately be talking about something other than their own original work and looking at the elements that attracted them in the various Greek originals that they adapted, but, if we do assume that each had an individual tone and ability, we can see that Terence offered later dramatists rather different dramaturgical models to those offered by Plautus. Terence is less interested in obscenity, than Plautus, he has fewer obvious comic routines either in the form of slanging matches or gloating over corporal punishments, and he seems to be more interested in plot than Plautus. There is perhaps a greater sense of morality in Terence's work and the romantic relationships are of interest in themselves rather than, as often in Plautus, an impetus for action by the intriguing slave, who is a much less central character in Terence. Another factor in Terence's art is that the characters he presents are almost all good people, he is not in the business of flaying vice and satirical comedy, which is of course one particularly important strand in the comic tradition that appears in, for example, the works of Aristophanes or the comedies of Ben Jonson (1572–1637 CE). Terence actually appears to like his characters and broadly speaking we are often asked to laugh with them rather than at them, a trait he shares with Shakespeare. The double plot in which two couples are generated out of an unpromising beginning is a technical device that enables him to give his characters a happy ending, so that there is much less emphasis on comic deflation in Terence than there is in many great comic writers. Even when Terence's old men try to thwart the young men's plans, they are presented as sensible and honourable, rather than lecherous.

In all these plays, love is presented as a disruptive force that must be channelled into socially acceptable forms. The most usual example of these forms is marriage because it represents metaphorically the place where a search for identity can end in the merging of two identities to create a single psychological entity which, as Hermia in the *Dream* describes her childhood friendship with Helena, is a kind of 'union in partition' (Shakespeare [1600] 2017: 3.2.210). Perhaps Shakespeare is more interested in this, perhaps Terence is more interested in the social unit. However, a crucial factor in the ways the plays work is the presentation of the different conditions of actual life in Rome or Greece as opposed to early modern England. These factors appear to severely inhibit Terence in his actual portrayal of women, as is also the case for Plautus and Menander. In ancient Greek and Roman comedy, the young women, the romantic heroines, sometimes do not appear at all and so the process of psychological adjustment has to be conveyed through the heroes' relationships with those who can influence the progress of their relationship with the heroine. In fact, in Terence's *Andria* (166 BCE) it is further complicated by the baby for whom arrangements must be made. One of the characteristics of Greek and Roman comedy is that babies figure to a much larger extent than they do in later comedies. This reflects the social conditions of Greece and Rome, and even their domestic architecture with its rooms around a courtyard, which form the natural indoors milieux of the heroines who are not often seen outside the house. Relatively often the heroine has had only one sexual encounter with the hero, often when she was at a festival and that sexual encounter has resulted in her becoming pregnant. This is not an easy convention for modern sensibilities to accept, since there is ultimately a problem in trying to deal with Romantic Comedies in which the heroines hardly appear and in which the 'romantic' relationship has begun with what we would now call a rape, that has itself led to an illegitimate baby. Despite the ancient authors' skill in introducing characters like the nurse who can voice Glycerium's fears in *Andria* we are largely confined to the hero's psychological development and the social repercussions of the romantic relationship rather than being offered any insight into how the heroine feels about either her initial predicament or her subsequent rescue. Underlying this may be the economic realities of status and marriage for both Greek and Roman young women. The male lovers may fight convention and insist on the validity of their view of experience in the face of others' views of what should be done, their commitment to the beloved may involve potential loss of status or wealth, or disgrace, dishonour and even death. However, this apparently foolhardy commitment to revolt is rewarded by reversal: it turns out that the beloved can confer new gifts on the lover because she is not who she is originally believed to be. This pattern is particularly obvious in Terence. Ultimately social duty and sexual preference turn out to be reconcilable.

Thus, although Terence's Romantic Comedy has many virtues and we can detect its influence in many later plays and their conventions, it inevitably suffers from the failure to show both partners in the romantic relationship on the stage. There are clearly sociological and cultural reasons why this was so, but it does represent a limitation even if Terence was able to chart the progress of romance through showing the male protagonist in relationship to other mainly male characters or in discussion with female servants, slaves, matrons and midwives. Shakespeare, on the contrary, had the freedom to show female characters on stage and that allowed him a greater depth in the presentation of the central romantic imbroglios.

English Romantic Comedy

Clearly there is no simple cause and effect relationship between the dramatic and theatrical practice of Menander and Shakespeare, since Menander's plays were lost at the time Shakespeare was writing but there is a much clearer relationship between the ways in which Plautus and Terence structured their plays and Shakespeare wrote his. From early in the sixteenth century, there was a renewed interest in Roman comedy that manifested itself in England with both staged revivals in Latin and English-language versions and reworkings. The Latin writers themselves were an important part of the school curriculum and Shakespeare clearly based *Comedy of Errors* (1594) in part on Plautus's play *Menaechmi*. There are also clear structural parallels between Terence's *Andria* and *Twelfth Night* (1601).

Similarly there are elements of the *Commedia dell' Arte* that find ready parallels with Shakespeare in stock figures such as heavy fathers and devices such as having two pairs of lovers at cross-purposes. Shakespeare also appears to display some knowledge of the *Commedia* tradition, particularly in *The Taming of the Shrew* (1591) and in adopting some of its characteristic terminology. The parallels between some of Shakespeare's plots and some *Commedia* scenarios probably point to a partially shared history rather than to a cause-and-effect relationship between genres and across centuries and countries. Clearly Romantic Comedy also shares many of the preoccupations of folk tales and fairy stories in terms of the quest for discovery of the true identity of the beloved, which often dissolves potential objections to a marriage by revealing apparent social disparities as actually being the result of mistaken assumptions about the apparently unsuitable partner. Many folk tales, fairy stories, myths and other narratives depend to a greater or lesser extent on the battles or quests of the lovers as they, often he rather than she, climb every mountain and perform every task until the ultimate goal of marriage is obtained. The assumption of the importance of heterosexual monogamy is key to the genre throughout most of its existence as is the preponderance of marriages that become possible only when an apparent disabling discrepancy between the social status of the lovers is shown to be false and/or paternal opposition is discredited. One of the characteristics of this patriarchal opposition is often the irrationality of that opposition.

Compared to tragedy, comic forms are relatively under-theorized and bedevilled by the elasticity of its capaciousness and its overlapping claims to formal qualities. Narrative comedy is potentially quite different from stand-up comedy, comic performance may easily exist outside the bound of comic narratives: the circus clown's comic antics and the plotting of a comic play may not always coincide in any meaningful sense, the stand-up routines of a Billy Connolly or a Phoebe Waller-Bridge may be differentiated both from each other and from dramatic comedy. Eliciting laughter may or may not be part of the comic enterprise and the mere presence of a 'happy ending' may or may not justify a work being called a comedy. And clearly Dante's use of the term 'comedy' in *The Divine Comedy* has little apparent relation to most modern usages of the word. If we take the satirical ancient Greek plays of Aristophanes as the first extant examples in a Western theatrical comic tradition, we can point to several elements that lurk behind or haunt some more modern forms of comedy. The emphasis on physical action, the beatings and broad humour, puns and caricature, flights of fancy and the castigation of villains are by no means unfamiliar and often co-exist with romantic strands in such forms as pantomime. On the other hand, the grotesque phalluses of Aristophanes have given way to more subtle manifestations such as the slap-stick and Mr Punch's truncheon.

I have chosen the plays for discussion in this book to illustrate the wide variety of forms that Romantic Comedy can take, paying attention in this introduction to the earliest extant forms of the genre in the work of Menander, Plautus and Terence, devoting some consideration to the social and theatrical conditions which limit the possibilities of the genre in their periods. Although the Roman comedies of Plautus and Terence mix and match elements of their no longer extant (except Menander) Greek originals, they seem to add one especially important element by providing the possibility of alternative objects/subjects of romantic love that open major possibilities in terms of plot and character development as well as expanding possible routes for multiple complications. Romantic Comedy has traditionally been defined in terms of a heterosexual couple becoming established in a recognized and socially sanctioned partnership, despite them having to overcome whatever obstacles are placed in their way by circumstances. Romantic Comedy is not, of course, restricted to the theatrical genre but occurs in many cultures and in many forms across history. Extant examples of ancient Greek prose romances such as Longus's *Daphnis and Chloe* and Achilles Tatius's *Leucippe and Cleitophon* demonstrate that romantic comedic plots were to be found elsewhere, as do later examples in medieval romance and in the *Commedia Erudita* and *Commedia dell' Arte*.[8]

Why comedy?

If comedy is involved with discussing how people do behave, should behave, should not behave and if it concentrates and offering models of behaviour to be avoided (satirical) or emulated as in the sentimental comedies of the eighteenth century or even just examined, then sexual relations offer a readily usable pattern of behaviour which can be adapted for many purposes. Sexual attraction and attitudes to sex provide useful instruments of analysis. Perhaps the near ubiquity of sex in comedy relates to comedy's supposed origins in fertility rites, perhaps those rites and comedy itself reflect the absolute centrality of heterosexual relationships in human existence. Fundamentally, we can say that, for most of history, without the procreative sex act there would be no comedy, because there would be no people to watch plays or do anything else, and that Romantic Comedy tends to concern itself with how people can be brought into a stable sexual partnership that can stand as a shorthand for prospective parenthood.

For the comic writer then, there is a great advantage to be gained from the use of some aspects of sexual relationships in comedy. The choosing of sexual partners has loomed very large in comedy, even if the process of choosing sexual partners has also been used as a vehicle for other elements. Perhaps, though, we might argue that there is a difference between sex and romance. Romance is a word with many possible meanings; it can describe genres (medieval romance), artistic movements (romanticism), content (Romantic Comedy). In many of its applications it has connotations of fantasy, untruth and improbability. It is often described as being opposed to something that we might call reality or as being concerned with trivia and of being light-hearted, in value systems where fact, truth, probability and seriousness are more highly regarded.

Given that all dramatic literature is a construct of words and implied actions, there is still often a distinction that is made between a work that approximates in some way to the texture of the lived world of experience and the work that does not attempt such an approximation. At certain historical moments and in certain types of drama, the relationship between the real world and the dramatic world may apparently become highly tenuous and this is where terms like romance and fantasy often come into play. We probably do not believe in the existence of fairies in quite the way that we believe in the existence of a bus route, nor do we quite accept the coincidences that are engaged in the plots of many Romantic Comedies, yet we can accept theatrical conventions in what is often termed the willing suspension of disbelief.

We can argue that there is an implied contract between us and the theatre company to believe that a particular actor is a supernatural character called Titania if we are watching *A Midsummer Night's Dream*. Presumably, this acceptance is ultimately concessive: we agree not to worry about certain facets of what is being presented to us in return for an implicit promise that our understanding of other important matters is being facilitated through us accepting these conventions. I believe in fairies for the duration of *A Midsummer Night's Dream* because it enables me to understand and enjoy the play better than if I choose not to believe. Audiences will readily affirm their belief in fairies in order to save Tinker Bell in J. M. Barrie's *Peter Pan* (1904). They do not, however, expect to be held to the same standards of veracity at that performance in the theatre that they would anticipate would obtain if they were giving evidence in a law court.

I believe that the fact that, for example, no-one can see through Viola's disguise in *Twelfth Night* partly depends on a willing suspension of disbelief from the audience, because without that suspension of disbelief the play simply would not work. Suspending disbelief is key to our pleasure. In terms of an implied contract between stage action and audience reaction, it is necessary for us to accept that Sebastian and Viola can be readily mistaken for another because, despite what we may know scientifically about male and female twins, unless the twins in the play are deemed to be indistinguishable from one another, there is no play at all. This may simply suggest that, unsurprisingly, drama is based on manipulating certain conventions and that some of these conventions may become outmoded, clichéd, conventional and of no practical utility. Presumably, it was once a new idea for a poet to compare his love to a red red rose. I would, however, suggest that the importance of this question of convention and particularly of the coincidence which is very much part of the tradition that underpins Romantic Comedy lies in the bargain made between the spectator and the theatrical event, the performance of Terence or of Shakespeare, that we will accept the improbable, the coincidental, the long lost children, the fairies, the twins who can be mistaken for one another, the boys who are also girls and the girls who are also boys and so on, only if it facilitates our understanding of the events being presented to us on stage. Perhaps the bargain might allow us to just enjoy the offered entertainment on its own terms, perhaps, more interestingly, the obviously unreal world of Romance and Romantic Comedy gives us some satisfaction because it is an imaginative and psychological projection of the hidden structures that underpin the real world, that everyday world of contingency in which the simple sequence of events inhibits our capacity to examine underlying causes and hidden connections that are obscured in the flux of everyday existence. And it is as it were a metaphoric way of engaging with happenings, issues and emotions that are not otherwise accessible.

The imaginative freedom of Romance may allow the writer to present the deep structure of an inner world which is normally hidden beneath the surface of the every day. This freedom and the ability to analyze factors that are normally concealed is one of the great strengths of dramatic media that are concerned with underlying patterns or truths rather than actual surfaces. In Romantic Comedy this inner world is usually psychological and, if the plays of Terence, for example, are to be seen as investigating inner psychological truths, we have to ask both what these truths are and how they have been presented. One persistent strand throughout the history

of Romantic Comedy is the prominence of characters who
are lost, often physically, but also often mentally. Shipwreck
and the loss of children figure prominently, woods are seldom
navigated without peril, quests appear to go hopelessly wrong.
Perhaps this process is easier in non-proscenium theatres
where the stage space may mutate from place to place without
the intervention of mimetic indicators of location.

Generally, people are in the wrong place at the wrong time
in all of these comedies, they are often deceived as to what is
actually going on either because someone is deliberately trying
to fool them or because they have managed to fool themselves.
People appear to be in love with people they aren't in love with
or are about to be married off against their wills. Identities
are by no means always clear nor, in Shakespeare's plays, are
sexual gender and human form fixed qualities, since Viola
becomes a man and Bottom becomes an ass.

One of the major psychological questions that all these
plays are concerned with is the question of identity and how
people find themselves and define themselves in social and
sexual relationships with one another: the majority of the
active sexual relationships between men and women in these
plays lead to an eventual arrangement of socially essential
and socially sanctioned couples, with most people apparently
more or less satisfied with who they end up with. The process
of affirming the couple, with all its assumptions of rightness
and happy ending, is used as an ideological benchmark for the
'natural' against which all the eccentricities of age, class and
gender can be attacked. The process of generating the couples is
a complicated one which occupies much of the dramatic time.
There are social repercussions in the other important elements
in Romantic Comedy, the apparent oppositions between love
and duty and between appearance and reality and the use of
a multi-stranded plot. The romantic relationship poses some
kind of challenge to authority, be it parental or social, but
in generating and fixing the couples the plays suggest that
true natures can be discovered in the course of the romantic
relationship. In its most basic form, the fact that a character
will disobey a father in order to marry another character is

an indication of a psychological emancipation from paternal and patriarchal authority into a world of relatively individual choice and decision making. As Richard Stockton Rand argues, in a discussion of young lovers in *Commedia dell' Arte* that is much more widely applicable to the young lovers in any Romantic Comedy:

> The terror of losing a 'self' they have not yet had time to discover is intensified by gushing sensations and hormonal changes that make it impossible for them to control their own bodies, let alone remember and adhere to prescribed codes of decorum. Their inability to control their own feelings, and the realization that they have little control over their romantic partner's feelings or any of the miscellaneous outside forces that dictate their destiny, are what characterise their inner crisis. Their needs and fears – conscious and unconscious – are what drive the scenarios.
>
> (in Chaffee and Crick 2015: 74)

Romantic love then offers individuals the opportunity to test the limits of their own characters by virtue of a clash of wills, often between generations, sometimes between potential beloveds. This clash of wills may well be robust and even painful, but holds out for both characters and audiences, promises of a greater understanding. For the audience, there is an opportunity to test our own understanding of human nature against the models offered to us on stage, but these models are not necessarily recommended to us, rather they are held up for scrutiny and judgement. So, if drama is at all concerned with organizing its material into a form that will encourage us to make judgements and draw analogies or contrasts with our own experience, then the phenomenon of love is a particularly useful vehicle for a far-reaching exploration of the nature of identity and of the individuals' relationship to society. This is expressed through the process of establishing the socially sanctioned couple or couples.

Love, however defined, can be a great vehicle for psychological discovery of one's own nature as well as that of the beloved. The limits of the self are discovered in the need to relate to another self: you must try to learn to trust the other, rather than assert your own self. Limits are being discovered, accommodations made, and in comedy the result is often expressed in the final union which creates the couple, a new unit out of what had been two previously separate individuals.

Marriage is important not only as a means of discovering social identity but also as a medium for the transmission of wealth and property by inheritance, which is one of the reasons why it is particularly important in comedy to find out who is whose child. This means that the most personal medium of transaction in human existence (sex), which stands at the opposite pole of experience to money (the most abstract means of transaction) can become an alternative means of expressing that transaction. There is ready source of comedy here since treating things like people and people like things is very widely recognized as a basis for comic effect. Moreover, the mechanism whereby sex is converted into money can readily embrace marriage, as well as the more obvious element of prostitution. By implication too, death figures in this equation since inheritance itself is a transaction dependent on death. The process of discovery that the lovers undergo may also be seen in social terms and appears, for a time at least, to threaten the social order before the couple is ultimately brought back within the norms of society. At the beginning of *A Midsummer Night's Dream*, Theseus cannot change the sharp Athenian law that her father Egeus demands be used against Hermia, but by Act Four the action of the play somehow enables him simply to override it because (implicitly) of the events of the night in the wood.

While Egeus makes his case for marriage as a patriarchal economic transaction, the action of *A Midsummer Night's Dream* encapsulates a contrary position against this tidy view of social and economic units and groupings. There is another facet of experience which must be considered, in the form of the power of an emotional commitment that makes one person prefer another. As Shakespeare says, there is no significant difference in rank, status or eligibility between Lysander and Demetrius, it just happens that Hermia wants Lysander not Demetrius. In these terms, the job of the dramatist writing Romantic Comedy is to investigate how duty and individual preference on one hand and social pressure and personal need on another can be accommodated within the available social framework. Ultimately the dramatist will do this by manipulating events so that these oppositions and discrepancies will be revealed as apparent rather than real, but in the course of the play the questions will be thoroughly investigated, and the audience, at least, will be made more aware of the need for social custom and practice to reflect individual aspiration. It is here that the value of the multiple plots becomes apparent since it can allow for an initial problem, complication and resolution within the dramatic structure. At its simplest, it means that the dramatist can organize material so that a discrepancy whereby two people who are both in love with a third, discover a fourth person that allows them all to pair off happily into couples. This can be complicated by cross purposes, mistaken identities, mistaken motivations and multiple potential lovers thus providing even more material for the dramatist to move from a double plot to add further elements that complicate the picture presented to us. Shakespeare's use of a third plot is another device which assists this process since third plots often provide an overt commentary on the romantic plots: the clothes and behaviour that Malvolio adopts in *Twelfth Night* after his tricking are a vivid physical demonstration of the absurdity of romantic pretensions; the rehearsal and performance of 'Pyramus and Thisbe' similarly undercuts the Athenian lovers' pretensions to any kind of tragic status in *A Midsummer Night's Dream*.

So, Shakespeare comments in various ways on the other romantic plots, in the difficulties the mechanicals encounter in trying to tell the story of Pyramus and Thisbe or in figures like Malvolio in *Twelfth Night*. Furthermore, while double plots are particularly good ways of dealing with mistaken identities, deceptions and intrigues, since they provide more characters to complicate situations, they also have the advantage of diffusing any empathic tendencies audiences might have to identify too closely with the protagonist. In tragedy, to put it crudely, we are often invited to identify with the leading character through whom the action is filtered and focused, but in comedy it is often more difficult to decide who the protagonist actually is. For example, in many comedies star actors have not been entirely clear about which role they should play. In comedy attention is much more likely to be divided more equally among the protagonists than it is in tragedy. As Samuel Taylor Coleridge put it, in tragedies 'the effect arises from the subordination of all to one' whereas in comedies 'the total effect is produced by a co-ordination of the characters, as in a wreath of flowers' where each individual flower contributes equally to the effect (Coleridge [1818] 1897). This means that, compared to tragedy, the doubling of plot in comedy means that there are many contenders for our attention, and we are likely to remain more distant and objective than we may in tragedy.

Comedies of Manners

In the Comedies of Manners which form a significant matrix for Romantic Comedy after the Restoration of King Charles II in 1660, the focus is not always on the potential married couples but often the romantic plots serve to highlight the potentially destructive patriarchal forces that determine so much of the social contexts of everyday life in their imagined worlds. In the material world of the Restoration, economic issues predominated over romantic attachment between individuals: estates had to be maintained, sons and daughters could be sold off to achieve a family's economic needs. There are complex economic and social factors underpinning the heavy emphasis on such issues in the drama of this period, related to the initial defeat of the royalists and their long absence from political power. In William Wycherley's *The Country Wife* (1676), William Congreve's *The Way of the World* (1700), Susanna Centlivre's *A Bold Stroke for a Wife* (1718) and in Oliver Goldsmith's *She Stoops to Conquer* (1773) the romantic plots serve to highlight the potentially destructive patriarchal forces that determine so much of the social contexts of everyday life. Centlivre explores the ways in which the social and legal codes militate against lasting romantic attachments by creating a nightmarish matrix of interlocking social obligations that obscure and inhibit the expression of true feelings. Here patriarchal power is literally embodied in the four guardians whose foibles virtually guarantee that the heroine can never find a potential husband who will be acceptable to all four. The formal devices allow Centlivre to expose the iniquities of patriarchal power through a romantic quest in which the hero must battle each of the four metaphorical dragons who guard the heroine. In *She Stoops to Conquer*, as I shall show, we are faced with many enactments of typical romantic obstacles, with questions of age and coming of age underlying the whole plot, and questions of (apparent) class difference and the patriarchal power to decide who is a suitable potential husband or wife, and who is not, looming large. In *She Stoops*, there may be potential romantic complications, although Tony Lumpkin is never a serious contender for the hand of Kate Hardcastle, but the key differences are located in clothes and superficial manners not in actual character so the potential barmaid/Kate Hardcastle/ Marlow triangle can be reduced easily enough to a pair and a pairing. Dramatic irony is a powerful factor here in distancing the potential tragic potential of mismatched dramatic couplings since the audience is aware throughout the play of the key factors that will defuse the apparent mismatches (here the existence of concealed information, such as the beloved's true identity and the actual age of a potential suitor). In *She Stoops to Conquer* the fathers are benevolent in their patriarchal intentions but require the romantic power of Kate's therapy to make their desired match possible.

The nineteenth century

In the nineteenth century Dion Boucicault's *London Assurance* (1841) exemplifies other aspects of the typical Romantic Comedy matrix with the exploration of contrasts between town and country values and how identities are constructed. However, by the end of the nineteenth century the position of women in society was changing as more women entered the work force and worked outside the home and this came to be reflected in so-called New Woman plays[9] and in changes to the ways in which the scenarios of potential Romantic Comedies came to be addressed. In both the twentieth century and in the contemporary period key legal and social changes have encouraged forms of drama in which hetero-normative and patriarchal assumptions have been challenged by more fluid approaches to dramaturgy.

Romantic Comedy against the grain

In Stanley Houghton's *Hindle Wakes* (1912) patriarchal consensus is challenged when their parents discover that a working-class woman has had a fling with a factory owner's son. The woman's parents and the man's father decide that the only way for the potential scandal to be closed down is for the couple to marry. Clearly this reflects the kind of fate that the patriarchal figures in Menander and Terence envisage for their offspring. However, the woman refuses the man, whom she doesn't see as a suitable husband, and leaves home to pursue an independent career. The first staging of the play excited controversy over its treatment of the theme precisely because the woman's repudiation of her traditionally assigned role is an indication of the extent to which traditional generic, gendered, class and societal values were under threat. Similarly in *Hobson's Choice* (1915), the figure of what might have been called a shrew in Shakespeare's time, comes to the fore as the character Maggie dominates her world, dispatches her would-be tyrant father, marries off her sisters, picks an apparently unprepossessing bootmaker from the literal depths of her father's subterranean workshop and transforms him into a suitable business and marriage partner, refuting many clichés along the way.

The opening up of society to new influences that characterized the twentieth century is reflected in the wider social ranges of heterosexual attractions in Romantic Comedies across class boundaries, the extension of the genre to homosexual relationships and the extension of its concerns to ethnic minorities. Whereas previously the idea of romantic relationships had been confined to young, socially and sexually attractive figures drawn mainly from a specific leisured and moneyed class, the form expanded to include interrupted or failed romantic relationships that were still comic but allowed the possibility that a good ending could be achieved by refutation of the traditional romantic synthesis in favour of an uncompleted action or an exploration of previously overtly unacknowledged aspects of the comic synthesis that had traditionally marked the culmination of the romantic explorations in the plays.

As Stanley Cavell has pointed out in *Pursuits of Happiness: The Hollywood Comedy of Remarriage* (1981), his analysis of the genre of Hollywood films that he has called 'Comedy of Remarriage', the wider availability and acceptance of divorce in the first half of the twentieth century in the United States and to a lesser extent in the United Kingdom added a whole new dimension to Romantic Comedy by opening up the genre to a world in which an initial romantic failure may be challenged and rerun with the initial protagonists overcoming the forces that drove them apart (often now located in their own psychology as well as or instead of external forces) to achieve the romantic synthesis that they were unable to reach first time round. Noël Coward's *Private Lives* (1930) dates from this period and perfectly illustrates the ways in which the liberalization of divorce legislation has led to the possibility of escape from the failure of the marital idyll once projected by the betrothals and weddings of traditional Romantic Comedy. Although Cavell specifically excludes the play from his new genre, the characters in *Private Lives* consistently and often consciously violate accepted social conventions, particularly those related to the sacredness of the marriage bond.[10] For each of the main protagonists, two weddings have not brought the promised bliss, so the hero and heroine try to achieve a new synthesis to deliver that promise by running away, back to what they hope will be a better future, informed by their previous mistakes with each other and with their now-discarded second partners.

Expanding the form

The investigation of customs may be searching enough to modify individual customs, but it scarcely results in revolutionary changes in the social order until much later in the twentieth and twenty-first centuries when the form of Romantic Comedy has had to expand to deal with some significant changes in the way that reality actually operates. Although the traditional comic matrix continued, and continues, to inform many plays, a growing number of works have chosen to pick out some aspect of that matrix for a more extended scrutiny that determines that the conclusion is one in which a traditional ending is not available. The influence of the failed matrix can be seen in the repeated disastrous attempts to form a family group in Shelagh Delaney's *A Taste of Honey* (1958) or the attempts by members of a forthcoming bridal party to enforce the rituals surrounding marriage on a prospective bridegroom (catatonic through drink) and bride (aware of the limitations represented by a traditional marriage) in Willy Russell's *Stags and Hens* (1978). Similarly, in Ayub Khan-Din's *East Is East* (1996) the complex patterns of relationships between a would-be Pakistani patriarch and his white English-born wife are played out against a series of comedic situations in which their children attempt to negotiate the pitfalls of mixed-race life in the 1980s. In the same author's *Rafta Rafta* (2007), adapted from Bill Naughton's 1963 *All in Good Time*, the exploration takes us beyond the conventional ending of Romantic Comedy into the grim practicalities of attempting to consummate a marriage in the face of crass interventions by the families with whom the young lovers must share their accommodation. The pitfalls of relationships in which one person is from one ethnic minority and another from a different ethnic minority provide the mainspring of Tanika Gupta's *Meet the Mukherjees* (2008) in which an explosive scrutiny of the sets of prospective in-laws sparks a searching exploration of barriers to romantic relationships between members of two different ethnic minorities. It is probably not unsurprising that Gupta should also have chosen to adapt *Hobson's Choice* into a study of an Asian-origin family business in the 1980s and explore persistent stereotypes about class and race through the matrix of a 1980s Lancashire small family business (2003).

While forbidden heterosexual love is at the root of Romantic Comedy, male homosexual love has long been taboo, because of legal prohibitions on homosexuality itself and because of theatrical censorship in the United Kingdom that was only abolished in 1968, both of which acted very forcibly against most attempts to treat homosexual issues at all. This was compounded, even after the abolition of censorship and the liberalizing of laws against male homosexuality, by the resurgence of illiberal attitudes that was represented by the notorious Clause 28 of the 1988 Local Government Bill.[11] It was against this background that a straightforward story of romantic love between underage boys, Jonathan Harvey's *Beautiful Thing* (1993), managed to charm audiences and critics alike. Exploration of themes and subtexts previously confined to the margins of the genre remain strong and it is perhaps fitting that David Eldridge's *Beginning* (2017) takes us back to the most fundamental issues of all. As the protagonists spar about whether they will have sex with one another, it is clear that the woman is looking to the man to impregnate her. The choice is between fathering a child or using a condom and although the situation is unresolved at the end of *Beginning* it does seem that they are opting for the possibility of procreation.

1

Shakespeare and Romantic Comedy

Contexts

Romantic comedies are about the social and psychological construction of identity. Of course, how a particular society structures its understanding of identity will differ according to particular historical circumstances but the process of choosing sexual partners offers clear routes into an exploration of how we think about ourselves and how we construct our sense of self. If the self is seen as constructed out of an array of social, mental, emotional and other facets, then trying to choose a beloved will depend on the extent to which any approach can accommodate another person's idiosyncratic characteristics into a particular mindset. If one potential partner is a vegan and the other is a carnivore, this is likely to be a major point of difference, particularly given the importance attached in most societies to communal eating as an index of social bonding.

William Shakespeare continues to occupy a central position in the history of Romantic Comedy in terms of the number of romantic comedies he wrote, their continued staging, the number of films and television productions of his comedies and the sheer weight of academic studies of many aspects of his achievements. We can identify a significant number of his plays as Romantic Comedies as well as several others whose status is rendered difficult for us by either the ways in which apparent romantic situations develop in problematic directions or due to changes in societal expectations since Shakespeare's time that open up the plays to scrutiny from new angles. Some of the plays are more straightforward than others in terms of presenting an apparently relatively simple romantic comedic dynamic such as *Comedy of Errors* (staged 1594), *Love's Labour's Lost* (1594), *A Midsummer Night's Dream* (1596), *The Merry Wives of Windsor* (1600), *As You Like It* (1600) and *Twelfth Night* (1601), some use a Romance template very directly (*Pericles*, 1608; *The Winter's Tale*, 1609; *Cymbeline*, 1610; *The Tempest*, 1611) but are not centred on a conventional Romantic Comedy strand.[1] Others contain within themselves a moment or moments that destabilize the possibility of Romantic Comedy and call it into question. *Measure for Measure* (1604) and *All's Well That Ends Well* (1605) are 'problem' plays precisely because they appear to follow a comedic arc until they bump up against something that is either demanded by or absolutely not required by the conventions of comedy. In *Measure for Measure*, Barnardine, the reprobate, who is inconveniently unwilling to be executed, and Ragozine, the conveniently deceased pirate, are both constructed by the play as meta-theatrical devices that underscore the challenges faced by both the plotters, substitute dramatists within the play, and the dramatist himself by drawing attention to the contrivances inherent not only in plots within plays but also in dramatic plotting itself. Similarly, *Measure for Measure* would pose an entirely different set of questions for an audience if Isabella answered one of the Duke's suggestions of marriage positively, or even at all. *All's Well That Ends Well* would end well enough, if Bertram did not choose to question how Helena was able to fulfil literally the folkloric challenge he had set for her of producing their baby without them having had sexual intercourse. Modern audiences also tend to be sceptical about the substitute bedmate tricks in these plays but there are other issues too at a naturalistic level in other plays. Lewis Carroll, for example, questioned Ellen Terry about why the whole Don John plot in *Much Ado about Nothing* (1598) could not have been nipped in the bud if Hero had behaved more rationally and attempted to refute his accusations (quoted in Shakespeare [1600] ed David L. Stevenson 1964: 138–9) and modern sensibilities have quailed at Beatrice's injunction to Benedick to 'Kill Claudio'. *Taming of the Shrew* (1591) has multiple problems about how to interpret much of the action and, of course, the treatment of Shylock tends to make *The Merchant of Venice* (1597) broken-backed even in the face of a whole final act that can be seen as a poetic attempt to cover a theatrical bad smell with verse deodorant. Neither *A Midsummer Night's Dream* nor *Twelfth Night* poses such major interpretative challenges, although the prolonged persecution of Malvolio can exert a problematic influence over a reading or staging of the play.

A Midsummer Night's Dream

Comedies were originally performed as part of festivals in both ancient Greece and Rome and structurally the connotations of festival, carnival and misrule are still persistently associated with them, even in recent works such as David Eldridge's *Beginning* (2017). The Shakespeare plays considered here are indebted to organizing principles that derive from festive practices and traditions around St Valentine's Day, Midsummer and Twelfth Night. The Romantic Comedy arc of *A Midsummer Night's Dream* is a very full rendition of the theme of romantic love, from the initial evocation of Theseus winning Hippolyta's love doing her injuries to an expansion of the traditional convention that the eventual marriages that conclude the action will be happy ever after into an interactive spell between audience and actors that binds the action in a circle and into a spell that wards off evil spirits – 'give me your hands' (Shakespeare [1600] 2017: 5.1.427). Moreover, the play itself chooses within its structure to enact one of the potential unhappy endings that would destroy the possibility of comic consensus. The story of Pyramus and Thisbe is one that recalls Lysander's narrative of the kinds of things that happen to true lovers and offers a burlesqued view of the tragic romantic impulse. Pyramus and Thisbe are star-crossed lovers doomed by parental opposition to seek fulfilment at Ninus's tomb where a dreadful beast of the night-time forest, similar to those previously invoked by Hermia in the first act, proves to be a grim reality that leads to a catastrophic denouement in which Thisbe, emulating or perhaps even foreshadowing Shakespeare's own Juliet in *Romeo and Juliet*, enacts the fate adumbrated in Lysander's speech. Metaphysical obstacles are reduced to prosaic reality in 'Pyramus and Thisbe' and its tragic end is subverted by the apparent ineptitude of the play script and the actors entrusted with its delivery.

At the beginning of *A Midsummer Night's Dream*, we have a very brief exchange, nineteen lines, that makes it clear that the proposed marriage between Hippolyta and Theseus does not arise from a conventional romantic courtship. There is a sharp contrast in diction and register between the two characters, as Hippolyta's much more abstract language, with its references to days and nights, the moon, a silver bow, heaven and solemnities (Shakespeare [1600] 2017: 1.1.7–11) giving way to Theseus's much more self-centred language ('I wooed thee with my sword, / And won thy love doing thee injuries; But I will wed thee in another key' (Shakespeare [1600] 2017: 1.1.16–8). Although the Athenian setting, the maturity of the characters and their mythological status may suggest both reason and stability, the language itself serves to undercut any easy assumptions about order. From the second half of the twentieth century productions have often emphasized discord between the protagonists by staging Hippolyta as some kind of prisoner (Griffiths 1996: 85–7). Into this brittle situation comes Egeus, Hermia's father and the prime exponent of patriarchal power, with complaints about his daughter's behaviour. A stock figure, he bristles with typical patriarchal arguments against his daughter and her beloved: she is his possession and his to dispose of as he sees fit, she is easily swayed by Lysander's arguments and his gifts and she is all too willing to disobey her father's commands. His list of Lysander's supposed seduction techniques firmly places Lysander as a textbook lover:

> This man hath bewitched the bosom of my child.
> Thou, thou, Lysander, thou hast give her rhymes,
> And interchanged love-tokens with my child.
> Thou hast, by moonlight, at her window sung,
> With faining voice, verses of feigning love,
> And stolen the impression of her fantasy;
> With bracelets of thy hair, rings, gauds, conceits,
> Knacks, trifles, nosegays, sweetmeats (messengers
> Of strong prevailment in unhardened youth),
> With cunning hast thou filched my daughter's heart,
> Turned her obedience, which is due to me,
> To stubborn harshness.
>   (Shakespeare [1600] 2017: 1.1.28–38)

Swiftly Shakespeare deploys the individuals that constitute the love triangle, Hermia and Lysander and Demetrius. Both Lysander and Hermia claim that Lysander is an eminently suitable candidate to marry her because he is as well derived as Demetrius, as rich or wealthier, and Hermia is in love with him. Lysander offers a non-viable solution that would square the triangle: 'You have her father's love, Demetrius. / Let me have Hermia's: do you marry him' (Shakespeare [1600] 2017: 1.1.93–4), clearly an impossibility, but Shakespeare then introduces a fourth name that promises the potential for an ultimate resolution. Helena was formerly the beloved of Demetrius before he switched affections to Hermia, but Shakespeare holds her appearance back from the audience until the initial situation is firmly established.

As Hermia says in her defiance of her father, Lysander and Demetrius are equal in rank, wealth and general eligibility, a point that has sometimes caused some difficulties for audiences who have found difficulties in telling them apart. Lysander and Demetrius have been seen as lightly differentiated (in 1856, the German Novelist Theodore Fontane was pleased that Charles Kean had clothed his lovers so that there was a visual reminder of who belonged with whom, Griffiths 1996: 154), thus reinforcing the apparently irrational choice of one over the other by both Egeus and Hermia. No one in the play disputes Hermia's claim that Lysander is just as eligible as Demetrius, but at this point in the play the patriarchal father's rights appear to be absolute. There was a debate in the period about the most appropriate way to deal with daughters who were unwilling to accept their fathers' plans for them, and Juliet Dusinberre (1975) has shown that one trend in contemporary thinking argued that the power of the father should be tempered by at least taking the daughter's wishes into account, but Egeus is a hard-liner in his determination to use his powers. Theseus offers Hermia a stark choice of death, becoming a nun or obeying her father and he is apparently powerless to do anything to extenuate the harshness of the Athenian law. While all this is going on Hippolyta is silent, but not necessarily passive in her reactions. Theseus's 'Come, my Hippolyta. What cheer, my love' (Shakespeare [1600] 2017: 1.1.122) retroactively implies that Hippolyta may have been actively indicating gesturally some response to the ongoing action that she has not voiced, and contemporary Hippolytas often indicate their sympathy for Hermia through their actions before they leave. Left alone, Hermia and Lysander relocate themselves verbally into another narrative context, that of the great romantic tradition, contrasting in their collaborative stichomythia with Egeus' virtuoso list of love tokens:

> **Lysander:** Ay me! for aught that I could ever read,
>   Could ever hear by tale or history,
>   The course of true love never did run smooth;
>   But either it was different in blood –
> **Hermia:** O cross, too high to be enthralled to low!
> **Lysander:** Or else misgrafted in respect of years
> **Hermia:** O spite, too old to be engaged to young!

Lysander: Or else it stood upon the choice of friends
Hermia: O hell, to choose love by another's eyes!
Lysander: Or if there were a sympathy in choice,
　　War, death, or sickness did lay siege to it …
Hermia: If then true lovers have been ever crossed,
　　It stands as an edict in destiny.
　　Then let us teach our trial patience
　　Because it is a customary cross,
　　As due to love as thoughts and dreams and sighs,
　　Wishes and tears, poor fancy's followers.
　　　　　　　　(Shakespeare [1600] 2017: 1.1.132–42, 150–5)

Lysander and Hermia's answer to the dilemma they find themselves in is to relocate themselves physically to Lysander's aunt's house seven leagues from Athens (an appropriately fairy tale distance) where 'the sharp Athenian law / Cannot pursue us' (Shakespeare [1600] 2017: 1.1.162–3). Traditionally Athens has been seen as a place of philosophy and enlightenment so there is an ironic quality to the action of the play in that the apparent home of logic and order that opens the action has to give way to a wild place that operates under the different principles of 'night rule'. In Romantic Comedies the corrective action that allows raw patriarchy to modulate into something gentler and more accommodating to the individual is often located outside the town, in a physical location that allows urban conflicts to be reworked in a different context where the carapace of civilization is scrutinized by more elemental factors and the underlying psychological dynamics can be revealed. As Richard Stockton Rand puts the general case, although he is dealing specifically with *Commedia dell' Arte* lovers:

Though Commedia Young Lovers were often portrayed as childish and immature, their journey represents a universal rite of passage that needs to be understood in a larger evolutionary context. Commedia lovers are more than cartoon characters. They are mythic archetypes working through fantasies and conflicts in the pursuit of sacred

love. Central to the young lovers' quest is their belief that
each human being has a soul mate, someone destined to
be their partner, someone with whom they can experience
wedded bliss and eternal fulfilment. ... As young lovers
see one another's insecurities, flaws, and inherent egotism,
their childlike fantasies of love are shattered and they are
made miserable by what they believe to be the death of love.
Yet it is the destruction of their fantasy that gives them an
opportunity to see the whole of one another and finding an
intimate connection they will need if they are survive long
enough to raise the next generation of young lovers.

(In Chaffee and Crick 2015: 77)

The arrival of Helena means that we now have been physically
introduced to the four young lovers who will provide the main
romantic entanglements of the play, but once it is established
that all four will be heading off to the wood, albeit with very
different motivations, the play changes direction completely
with the switch to the casting of 'Pyramus and Thisbe', the
play within the play. For the audience, this is a major change
of perspective from the rhyming couplets that end Act One
Scene One to the prose of the next scene, from aristocratic
characters in the ducal court to carpenters and weavers and to
a scenario that has scarcely been mentioned before. This scene
not only introduces the amateur actors and draws potentially
uncomfortable attention to some of the issues that bedevil all
actors, but also offers a brief insight into the way that the story
of *A Midsummer Night's Dream* will develop: Bottom and
Flute are cast as a lover (Pyramus) and his beloved (Thisbe)
whose attempts to meet at night in a deserted place do not go
well, while three of the other four actors are cast as parents
(Thisbe's mother and father and Pyramus's father) who will
ultimately not appear at all in the play of 'Pyramus and Thisbe'
that we see rehearsed or performed.

Once this scene ends, we might expect to get back to the
lovers but instead we are relocated again. This time into a
night-time wood that is peopled with supernatural characters.

The king and queen of the fairies, Oberon and Titania, are deep in a marital quarrel over who should take charge of an Indian boy and, according to Titania, their discord has even affected the weather. From the Romantic Comedy point of view, theirs is the second relationship between presumably mature adults (we should perhaps be wary about being too definitive about the age or psychology of fairies) that is flawed, and the action of the play will show how Oberon and Titania arrive at a reconciliation. In the theatre, it has become customary in the last fifty years or so to use doubling to reinforce the idea that the two couples represent different facets of essentially the same pair with Theseus and Hippolyta representing the Athenian, supposedly rational, daytime social world, and Oberon and Titania representing a more irrational, visceral, tempestuous world of atavistic supernatural conflict. This approach has many advantages in terms of providing a rationale for why Theseus is in a position in Act Four to override Egeus's objections whereas he was hamstrung by the law in Act One.

In the case of the *Dream*, the four lovers enter the wood certain of their own identities and their place in the social structure but each of them will be subjected to a destructive set of processes in which their old certainties are assaulted (Figure 1) until they finally reach a new cooperative understanding of how their reality is constructed that allows them to escape their old individualistic ways of seeing the world. As Richard Stockton Rand puts it, again talking specifically of *Commedia* lovers, but in terms that can be usefully applied to such characters in the wider world of Romantic Comedy:

> The beating heart of the young lover is clipped by conflicting impulses and paralyzing contradictions. While attempting to control their emotions and retain some semblance of autonomy, they yearn to shed all restraint and merge with their lover. Unable to tolerate the tension of these opposing forces, the lovers' carefully crafted personas begin to fall apart. … Whether they are swept up in romantic ecstasy, consumed with jealousy, or crushed by perceived betrayal,

their emotional swings – *experienced alternately or in rapid succession* – propel the action and make them both heart rending and farcical.

(In Chaffee and Crick 2015: 75)

Figure 1 A Midsummer Night's Dream, *by William Shakespeare, directed by Dominic Dromgoole. Sarah MacRae (as Helena), Olivia Ross (as Hermia), Joshua Silver (as Demetrius), Luke Thompson (as Lysander) quarrelling in the wood. Shakespeare's Globe Theatre, London, UK; 29 May 2013. Credit: Pete Jones/ArenaPAL; www.arenapal.com*

In the night-time wood of the *Dream* the senses can no longer be relied on and apparently settled relationships are shattered. Language itself breaks down and so does individual corporeal identity. Far from being simply the road to safety, the wood is a dangerously inclusive place that frays individual identities. Demetrius's unfortunately now obsolete pun on madness and the forest when he declares that he is 'wood within this wood' (Shakespeare [1600] 2017: 2.1.192) is indicative of the ways in which what goes on in the wood will disrupt apparent certainties and fragment the individuals' sense of self. While both Demetrius and Lysander will, under the influence of Puck's magic, come to love Helena, neither Hermia nor Helena will be cushioned by supernatural intervention as they attempt to negotiate their new situations. Shakespeare chose to differentiate his female protagonists in the *Dream* to a much greater extent than the men, emphasizing their differences in stature and hair colour whereas the men are not only interchanged by Puck's injudicious use of the magic flower but even lose their identities completely when Puck assumes their vocal identities. From a situation in which Lysander tries to press his suit on a resolutely chaste Hermia to one in Helena wakes him from his sleep, the plot rapidly deploys into what could be described as the mistakes of a night as Puck misinterprets the evidence on stage before him. The audience know that Lysander and Hermia are a true couple but Puck, unaware that there are two couples in the wood believes that the male Athenian he sees is Demetrius and ascribes their chaste separation to the Athenian man's refusal to accommodate the sleeping woman rather than to Hermia's unwillingness to share a sleeping place with Lysander.

As an example of two pairs of young lovers sorting out their differences cooperatively (even if under the influence of magic), *A Midsummer Night's Dream* is a refutation of overbearing patriarchal demands, albeit mediated by a gentler form of patriarchy in Theseus's final decision to override Egeus, that is also accompanied by a sorting out of the trials of married lovers (Oberon and Titania) who may in turn be seen to represent the (unstated) issues that need to be resolved between Theseus and Hippolyta before they can be married. All of this is accompanied by a presentation of another alternative fate for lovers in the rehearsal and presentation of the very tragical mirth of the love story of Pyramus and Thisbe. In the *Dream* there is one actual father Egeus and one father mentioned (old Nedar) but, despite the strength of other patriarchal forces and figure, the actual fathers are effectively reduced in power by the outcome of the action. Interestingly, Egeus is not always present in Act Five (and to my knowledge old Nedar, Helena's father, has only made one appearance, in the last act of Granville Barker's 1914 production. See Griffiths 1996: 194).

A Midsummer Night's Dream deftly melds many initially disparate elements into a dizzyingly self-reflexive exploration of the potential of Romantic Comedy. In the context of Theseus and Hippolyta's forthcoming marriage, two pairs of young lovers sort out their differences in a refutation of overbearing patriarchal demands. However, as Simone de Beauvoir points out in a discussion that is not about Shakespeare's Helena, that character encapsulates something more disturbing than simply an infatuated woman:

> [The] religion of love is an 'idolatrous love,' Simone de Beauvoir argued in Le Deuxième Sexe (1949), deceiving women with the belief that they can remedy the effects of their social and economic dependency by making themselves essential to a superior power, to a demigod a transcendent freedom – in other words, to a man. Here begins the female lover's characteristic self-abasement, which flirts with masochism, collusion and bad faith. Such is the woman's devotion to her partner's freedom, Beauvoir observes, that the man's inescapable mediocrity, his inevitable uncertainty, his irresistible inertia and facticity or as much a torment to her as his power to command and to possess: 'she wakes

him up simply to keep him from sleeping', for her 'god must not sleep lest he become clay, flesh'. Meanwhile the deity to whom she sacrifices herself grows tired of his lover's selflessness, and hard as she tries to please him the more he loses interest: 'Giving herself blindly, woman has lost that dimension of freedom which had first made her fascinating. The lover seeks his reflection in her; but if he begins to find it altogether too faithful, he gets bored. It is, again, one of the loving woman's misfortunes to find that her very love disfigures her, destroys her; she is nothing more than this slave, this servant, this too ready mirror, this too faithful echo.'

(Beauvoir quoted in Bowring 2019: 3–4).

While the four Athenian lovers conduct themselves in ways which bear out the general applicability of de Beauvoir's strictures, simultaneously a squabbling established pair of lovers (Oberon and Titania) engage in a fierce marital war whose battles and ultimate reconciliation are widely seen as working out very similar issues to those that need to be resolved before Theseus and Hippolyta can be married, a factor reinforced by current casting decisions that usually double the actors playing the roles. All this is accompanied by an enactment of an alternative fate for would-be lovers in the rehearsal and presentation of the 'very tragical mirth' of the love story of Pyramus and Thisbe. Pyramus and Thisbe feature as the protagonists of a story in the Roman poet Ovid's *Metamorphoses* (8 CE) and in many subsequent serious treatments by medieval writers, including Giovanni Boccaccio, Geoffrey Chaucer and John Gower. Shakespeare himself followed the pattern of the story via a later branch of the tradition in his *Romeo and Juliet*, thereby essentially supplanting Pyramus and Thisbe as tragic figures in English with Romeo and Juliet. The mechanicals reduce the metaphysical story of metamorphosis to the resolutely physical in their attempts to stage a story that parallels and parodies

the adventures of the four lovers of the *Dream*. The impetus
towards death in the Pyramus and Thisbe story parallels that
of the Athenian lovers in the wood ('Either death or you I'll
find immediately' [Shakespeare [1600] 2017: 2.2.160]) but it
is contained and defused both by the incompetence of Quince's
troupe of actors and the deliberately poor quality of the
writing in the play of 'Pyramus and Thisbe' which transforms
the potentially tragic into the bathetic (although some modern
performances have found genuine pathos in some aspects of
the final performance, particularly Thisbe's death speech). In
performance, 'Pyramus and Thisbe' often lacks subtlety and
actors and directors indulge in grotesqueries of all kinds, but
Shakespeare has incorporated a number of moments that refer
directly to the storylines of the four lovers that, if heard, can
help to bind the apparently discrete worlds of the play together.
Often, the hysterical mood both onstage and in the audience
during the performance of 'Pyramus and Thisbe' can obscure
the fact that there are lines about Limander (a mistake for
Lysander) and Helen in the text of the playlet that suggest that
the mechanicals are not unaware of the possibility of making
a graceful contemporary allusion to their patrons. Similarly
Theseus's remark during the performance that Pyramus might
recover and prove an ass can be used to provoke a sense of
meta-theatricality but often fails to be heard in the face of
reactions to the performance of 'Pyramus and Thisbe'.

Lysander and Hermia consciously identify themselves
with examples of the great tradition of love such as Pyramus
and Thisbe, and they express beliefs and act in ways that are
consistent with those of the *Commedia* lovers in Richard
Stockton Rand's formulation:

> The catalyst for the young lovers' dramatic journey is the
> life force and interpersonal dynamism generated by the
> shared fantasy of 'true' love. This energy enables lovers to
> respond to changing circumstances, overcome obstacles,
> gain insight into themselves and the world around them, and
> learn life lessons they will need on the next journey. Though

we laugh at their dilemmas and overreactions, Commedia Young Lovers are experiencing the same emotions and are motivated by the same hopes and fantasies that have motivated all young lovers.

(In Chaffee and Crick 2015: 78)

Lysander and Hermia may use their adherence to the great tradition of love as a paradoxical way of asserting their uniqueness, but Puck has a more mundane version of their situation that he voices when bringing the four lovers together again: 'Jack shall have Jill, / Nought shall go ill, / The man shall have his mare again, and all shall be well' (Shakespeare [1600] 2017: 3.2.461–3). This usage of Jack and Jill pre-dates the first known occurrence of the nursery rhyme and suggests the coupling of two prosaic names in contrast to the esoteric, mythological, and aristocratic connotations of Hermia, Helena, Demetrius and Lysander.

A Midsummer Night's Dream provides a significant map of many aspects of the Romantic Comedy landscape. That map is currently being further enhanced by recent developments in approaches to casting and directorial choices that have, for example, given traditionally male roles to female performers and vice versa. Generally, since 1660 the majority of characters have been played by what have historically been deemed to be actors of the appropriate gender, male characters by male actors, female characters by female characters. Recent notable exceptions to the general rule have included an all-male *Twelfth Night* at the Globe in 2002 or Fiona Shaw as Richard II, Vanessa Redgrave as Prospero, Maxine Peake as Hamlet (emulating Sarah Bernhardt) or Ian McKellen's age and gender neutral *Hamlet*. The one major generic exception to this rule has been pantomime, where the cross-gender casting of the pantomime dame and the principal boy is routine. In the *Dream* the fairies have been a significant exception with both Oberon and particularly Puck sometimes played by actresses rather than actors, but latterly cross-gender casting has extended to take in a much wider variety of characters. Such inclusive

casting may pose challenges for an experienced theatregoer
who may have come to expect that, as Keir Elam put it, citing
Groucho Marx's bewilderment at what turned out to be just
scratches on Julie Harris's legs, that everything on a stage can
and should be assumed to be a sign (Elam 2002: 8). At present
there are a range of potentially conflicting inclusive practices
that co-exist in the theatrical world in which the spectrum of
what may or may not be motivated and open to interpretation
in terms of the assignment of performers to roles is itself open
to question.

Historically, *A Midsummer Night's Dream* has had a
very chequered theatrical life and many apparently recent
innovations have some parallels with past practices. The
now almost universally favoured doubling of Theseus and
Hippolyta with Oberon and Titania was first mentioned in
print in 1660 but resurfaced in the 1960s before Peter Brook's
1970 staging cemented the practice as one that was both
economically useful and thematically resonant. Sometimes, in
contemporary theatre productions, new approaches to casting
have paid particular dividends. In the case of the *Dream*,
the most notable example of cross-dressing was perhaps
when the comedian Dawn French played Bottom in a 2001
production where the idea was that the mechanicals were
wartime Women's Institute members, and their only male
participant was Flute. Early Modern theatre used boy actors
for young female parts, so it is perhaps logical for Quince to
give Thisbe to Flute whose claims to have has a beard coming
are often mocked in performance. Generally, however, until
recently performers of the mechanicals have mainly stuck
within what we might term a naturalistic approach to casting,
except in a few cases such as French's. Clearly such casting
practices invite audiences to consider meta-theatrical issues
and swapping Bottom's gender so that his actor is a woman
can add extra potency to the modern practice of emphasizing
not only Bottom's ass head but also his ass penis. In Emma
Rice's 2016 Globe production the mechanicals were supposed
to be Globe staff led by a formidable Rita Quince and in other

productions that used women to play the mechanicals the traditional practice of Starveling being played by a tall thin man has been extended to having him played by a tall thin woman.

Perhaps the most challenging example of a different approach to casting leading to some new insights occurred in 2016 when Rice decided, with her dramaturg Tanika Gupta, to change Helena's gender so that she became Helenus. The quartet of lovers poses their own challenges in terms of casting and behaviour. Generally speaking they have been treated as two women and two men, but they have also been shown as liable to behave erratically if left to their own devices without fairy intervention: Nevill Coghill's quartet in 1945 lay down far apart in 3.2 'but Puck made a gesture and they rolled together into their right pairs', earlier in the play John Caird's 1989–90 Puck had to divert the waking Demetrius away from Lysander and towards Helena (Griffiths 1996: 175 and 159). Clearly changing the gender of a character who has previously been conceived of as being female to be a man, as in the case of Helena becoming Helenus made a difference to the way in which the play worked and, judging on the evidence of the critics, how audiences perceived it. As Maxie Szalwinska saw it:

> One of Rice's coups, along with dramaturg Tanika Gupta, is to turn Helena into Helenus, who is Hermia's gay best friend until her beloved Lysander starts to pursue him. This change makes complete sense: the scorning of Helenus by his shame-filled former boyfriend Demetrius (Ncuti Gatwa), in favour of a more socially palatable match clicks into place. Ankur Bahl's Helenus, touched with camp but not weighed down by it, alternates between heartsore fragility and strength.
>
> (*Sunday Times*: 15 May)

Similarly Paul Taylor drew attention to 'a lovely moment in the forest where the three men absently share lip gloss and the excluded Hermia's gay-best friend relationship with Helenus unravels with wholly convincing bitterness' (*Independent*: 6 May). If, however, the female part simply been played by a man, the effects might have been very different.

Figure 2 A Midsummer Night's Dream, *by William Shakespeare, directed by Nick Hytner. Gwendoline Christie (as Titania) presiding over the quarrel between Paul Adeyefa (as Demetrius), Isis Hainsworth (as Hermia), Kit Young (as Lysander), and Tessa Bonham Jones (as Helena). Bridge Theatre, London, UK; 4 June 2019. Credit: Manuel Harlan/ArenaPAL; www.arenapal.com*

At the Bridge Theatre in Nicholas Hytner's 2019 production, in which a significant part of the audience occupied an area that they shared with the action and had fairies flying above their heads:

The magic passion flower is bandied about in a way that allows just about every kind of sexuality to get a look-in and psychological sense is made of Theseus's new-found sexual tolerance because he and his fairy counterpart Oberon, it is implied, are the same people living in parallel universes. The same is true of [Gwendolyn Christie's] Hippolyta and Titania who both liberate their worlds from a patriarchal form of oppression.

(John Nathan, *The Jewish Chronicle*: 13 June 2019)

Although Nathan does not consider how this doubling has worked elsewhere, over some fifty years, this decision has clearly liberated a thematic spine that was implicit within the play. In Hytner's production there was a considerable amount of stress on what Michael Billington described as 'male power hunger' in *The Guardian* (11 June 2019). Hytner had reassigned significant chunks of Titania's lines to Oberon and Oberon's to Titania. This swapping of lines opened up a further riff on the potential for polymorphous sexuality when Oberon ended up with the translated Bottom, but, since each character was played by an actor whose gender corresponded to that usually assigned to the role this meant that Oberon became infatuated with a male Bottom. Oliver Cris, who played Oberon, was also doubling up as a patriarchal Theseus whose Hippolyta first appeared in a glass cage wearing clothes that reminded some critics of Amish dress and others of Margaret Atwood's *The Handmaid's Tale*. As Billington remarked, 'The payoff comes when, returning to Theseus, Chris is forced to soften his sexual authoritarianism by recalling his dalliance as Oberon with a male donkey.' Billington thought that the director was aiming 'to question the idea of a rigid, binary sexuality' that led him to have Lysander and Demetrius, as

well as Hermia and Helena, snogging each other in the midst
of what is meant to be a fierce fight in the forest (Figure 2).
Other critics picked up on the 'gender-bending antics' and the
four lovers enjoying 'a little same sex love' (Patrick Marmion,
Daily Mail: 12 June 2019) or, like Paul Taylor opined that
'transgressive sex is the heart of Shakespeare's summer
staple—boys in love with the wrong girls, girls in love with
the wrong boys, women in lust with donkeys. And it remains
at the centre of Nicholas Hytner's immersive approach, which
unleashes an exuberant burlesque spectacle of genderqueer
transformation and desire' in which Hytner's reassignment
of lines 'illuminates the abusive power dynamic at the centre
of a comedy steeped in images of male sexual violence and
stays entirely true to its radical spirit'. Oberon and Bottom's
dalliance did cause him to note that Oberon's translation
might be considered problematic: 'From butch-as-hell hippy,
he becomes a highly strung male diva with a possessive,
neurasthenic passion for his new chum. This might seem to
sail uncomfortably close to gay stereotypes if it weren't for the
affectionate way the production ridicules camp convention'
(*The Independent*: 12 June 2019).

In some cases the actor playing a role may not be of the
gender or race normally associated with that role, but no
particular significance appears to have been perceived by
critics. In Hytner's production, Demetrius and Lysander
were both played by BAME actors and the two women by
white actresses, and in a later production of the *Dream*,
at the Globe in 2019, the fact that Egeus was played by
a black woman appeared not to have any intended or
perceived effects on the outcomes within the world of the
play. Neither race nor gender was activated as an issue here
and the four lovers were all BAME actors. Similarly in this
production Bottom and the mechanicals were played by
black and mixed-race women (with the exception of a white
male Flute) without attracting any attention to questions of
race or gender.

Twelfth Night

After the remarkably inclusive ending of *A Midsummer Night's Dream*, *Twelfth Night* concludes with a much smaller group of characters who are much less representative of the whole social spectrum that the play has explored beforehand. In *Twelfth Night* two twins, Viola and Sebastian have been shipwrecked on the coast of Illyria, each unaware that the other has survived. Viola, disguising herself so that she looks like her brother, heads off to the court of Orsino where, as Cesario, she soon becomes a favourite courtier. Orsino sends him/her off to woo Olivia, who falls for him/her. Meanwhile Sebastian is also heading for Orsino's court and the comic mechanism is primed for a series of mistakes and misdirections as both twins become involved in various cross-purpose intrigues until eventually it is revealed that Cesario is actually a woman and can marry Orsino while Sebastian has earlier married Olivia who believes him to be Cesario. While much of the action is concerned with bringing these four young people together in a socially sanctioned agreement, the threat posed to the harmony by the outsider, Malvolio, who is Olivia's steward, is continued right up to the last scene. This outsider has a substantial part to play in the action as a whole, figuring large in the subplot and wanting to be assimilated into the dominant group. Here the mood is different to the ending of the *Dream* where no characters remain outside the comic pattern. Malvolio's last words are 'I'll be revenged on the whole pack of you!' (Shakespeare [1623] 2008: 5.1.371) and he is an outsider who cannot be contained within the pattern of the comic resolution, but who casts a long shadow over it.

Twelfth Night apparently concludes in the approved manner of Romantic Comedy with families reunited, two couples married offstage and one couple about to be married onstage, but the shadows cast by Malvolio and even by Feste's final song can mitigate against seeing the ending as unproblematic. Similarly, so does the fact that the traditional romantic cross-purposes are being continued visually in Orsino's insistence that Cesario remains dressed as a man for the rest of his/her time on stage. Unlike *A Midsummer Night's Dream*, patriarchal power is literally absent throughout the play: Theseus, Egeus and the absent Nedar have been replaced in *Twelfth Night* by an absence of patriarchs. There are no actual fathers present in the play: the twins' father is either dead or alive wherever they originally came from and both Olivia and Orsino operate as autonomous independent figures at the head of their respective households. In Olivia's case her absent (dead) brother, delinquent uncle and arriviste steward, exert almost nothing in the way of patriarchal power, despite Toby and Malvolio's efforts. Similarly Orsino's family are non-existent within the world of the play.

Three of the four prospective young lovers are beset by doubts and difficulties of their own making during the course of the play as they pursue impossible or forbidden goals, while the fourth, Sebastian, finds himself in a disturbed world that he swiftly moves to take advantage of. By the end of the play Toby has married Maria and Sebastian has married Olivia, but Toby and Maria's wedding makes no impact on the denouement. Disguise, as Viola says, is a sin and that ties in with contemporary social fears exacerbated by concerns about the trained young men who played female parts such as Olivia and Viola. Much energy has rightly been spent on trying to tease out what expectations and responses contemporary audiences might have had of these actors and of their playing but unsurprisingly there is no conclusion about the ramifications of the practice. At the very least we can probably assume that at certain points in the action audiences were encouraged by both play texts and stage pictures to be aware that what they were apparently seeing was more complex than a simple mimetic reproduction of a character's supposed gender and at these moments there was likely to be a frisson of recognition that conventional extra-theatrical boundaries were being transgressed.

Moreover, *Twelfth Night* ends with Feste alone onstage to sing his final song. Although we have had three couples established, Feste sings a song about the harshness of nature and the difficulties of human life that leaves us with a number of unanswered questions about the future, again in contrast to the world of *A Midsummer Night's Dream*. In the *Dream* the characters reach something that could legitimately be described as the right result, as couples are established, the play within the play is performed and marriages are blessed. In *Twelfth Night* there is a much greater stress on the pains of love rather than on the rewards of love. The stage picture of three men and one woman has, until very recently and with changes in the law permitting same-sex marriages, suggested an imbalance in the face of accepted social norms. We may have been expected to accept the substitution of the male twin for the female one as shorthand for a resolution of the complexities of the plot, but equally the play may not have convinced us that Olivia and Sebastian and Orsino and Viola are a necessary couple of couples, in even the same way as Demetrius and Helena are in the *Dream*. Unlike the *Dream*, *Twelfth Night* does not take responsibility for all its characters: Maria and Toby are absent at the end. and little charity is expended on Andrew, let alone Malvolio.

Disguising herself as a man gives Viola a freedom of action that is not available to a conventionally dressed woman. Her reasons for assuming disguise are rather sketchy. She asks the Captain, her saviour from the shipwreck, some questions about Illyria and Orsino and then simply declares:

> Conceal me what I am, and be my aid
> For such disguise as haply shall become
> The form of my intent. I'll serve this duke.
> Thou shalt present me as an eunuch to him.
> It may be worth thy pains for I can sing
> And speak to him in many sorts of music,
> That will allow me very worth his service.
> What else may hap to time I will commit.
>   (Shakespeare [1623] 2008: 1.2.50–7)

Viola's disguise lacks the overt rational basis of Rosalind's in *As You Like It* or Portia's in *The Merchant of Venice* and she is much less happy in her role than those other heroines, since she almost immediately finds herself beset with apparently intractable problems associated with the very fact of her disguise. That disguise is in fact necessary in bald plot terms since no disguise means no play, but also in thematic terms since it opens up for us a whole pattern of people who are not what they play. All the main characters – Orsino, Olivia, Viola, Sebastian, Malvolio and Feste – are actively involved in playing roles and it is tempting from that to go on to see the play in fairly conventional terms as one that deals in dramatic irony, that familiar gradual narrowing of a gap between the characters' own perceptions and our greater knowledge of events. To some extent, and at a mechanical level, this is true in the sense that the facts behind the various tricks are revealed at the end and the characters arrive at a level of awareness of those facts that matches ours. Cesario eventually acts as a kind of moral tutor to both Olivia and Orsino as his/her adopted androgyny permits him/her to move literally between the two worlds of the play. And here, unlike in the *Dream*, there is no redemptive green space to apply a necessary corrective. Puck's 'night rule' is matched by Toby's failure to keep time but nature has dwindled into a box tree. Plans are made but never come to fruition and the subtitle points the way.

However, there is an issue in that the actions of the play do not seem to suggest a necessary growth in psychological understanding that matches the characters' understanding of more facts than they did at the beginning. The play takes a group of people away from a set of attitudes, but it does not show a full growth into a new understanding. Even in the *Dream,* where the four lovers know almost nothing of the process they have undergone, we have the benefit of observing that process and therefore we have a fairly secure base for judgement that some things have genuinely changed. In *Twelfth Night* there are many more questions left without complete answers. Shakespeare is very inclusive and confident in the ending of the earlier play with its reconciliation of Oberon and Titania coupled with the blessing of the marriages of the mortals whose progeny will be blessed by the fairies' final spell. In contrast, take Orsino in *Twelfth Night*: he is the Duke, he has the first and last words of the play, Viola has apparently heard that he is noble, he was a soldier once and he manages to keep order in his court. Yet our impression when we actually see him is surely that he is somewhat of an adolescent in love with the idea of being in love. His very first speech of the play gives us a very strong idea of him as a conventional moody lover: 'If music be the food of love, play on,/Give me excess of it' followed five lines later by 'Enough, no more!/'Tis not so sweet now as it was before' (Shakespeare [1623] 2008: 1.1.1–2, 7–8) and then by the generalization that love makes even valuable things full rapidly into abatement and low price even in a minute. The first scene suggests that he has fallen in love with Olivia almost as part of the prescribed education for a courtier and that he is now pursuing a rigorous training programme of listening to music and as he says at the end of scene one lying on 'sweet beds of flowers' since 'Love-thoughts lie rich when canopied with bowers' (Shakespeare [1623] 2008: 1.1.39–40), with Shakespeare using the conventional couplet ending of the scene to undercut Orsino's sentiments and point up their ridiculousness. Shakespeare carefully refrains from showing us very much about the court. We only see Valentine and Curio briefly before Cesario arrives to dominate proceedings, but it is clear that Curio has ideas about how his ruler should behave including hunting not loving. Orsino is presented as a man with an obsession which is taking over his life completely, but this obsession is almost entirely theoretical. In sending his messengers off to woo on his behalf he is taking no risks since he can get on with the business of luxuriating in being in love and not having to face any practical problems in dealing with his beloved in person.

Suffering can be a significant part of the comedic process for the individual lovers. That suffering is often mitigated for audiences by the operation of dramatic irony or the fact of a discrepant awareness between audiences and characters. We know that there are two male and two female lovers from quite early in the first scene of *A Midsummer Night's Dream* and the fact of Sebastian's existence and his first appearance relatively early in *Twelfth Night* offers us a potentially beneficial rearrangement of the apparent triangle in that play into the necessary square of couples in due course. Our greater knowledge of the romantic possibilities allows us to discount the power of some of the pain involved in the cross-purposes of Orsino, Olivia and Viola. However, love is painful in this play. Both Olivia and Viola begin with the pains of familial love for dead brothers, Olivia, like Viola, is hiding behind a pretence, in her case the literal veil that hides her face, because she is in mourning for her brother for seven years. Orsino, when told this by Valentine, sees it as a solid proof of her fine nature 'O, she that hath a heart of that fine frame / To pay this debt of love but to a brother, / How will she love when the rich golden shaft / Hath killed the flock of all affections else / That live in her' (Shakespeare [1623] 2008: 1.1.32–6). Others might see it as a case of the lady protesting too much. and we may note that our actual experience of Olivia onstage is quite different from the way that she is reported to us. Shakespeare skilfully holds back the first actual physical appearance of Olivia until some 300 lines into the play. By then we have heard about her from Valentine and Orsino, the Captain, Toby, Andrew, and Maria and finally Cesario. When she does appear in person, Olivia's first line is 'Take the fool away' (Shakespeare [1623] 2008: 1.5.35), but it only takes Feste about 30 lines to convince her that she is overdoing her mourning zeal and she is soon talking more naturally with her retinue.

Olivia's rebuke to Malvolio 'O, you are sick of self-love, Malvolio, and taste with a distempered appetite' (Shakespeare [1623] 2008: 5.1.86–7) is key to our understanding of the obstacles to the course of true love in the play. It is clearly applicable not only to Malvolio but also to Orsino and even to Olivia herself. Yet, even at this very early stage she is presented as more clear-sighted and active than Orsino. Even if Shakespeare chooses to make her come to seem foolish, it is because her sudden catastrophic realization of her own nature when she falls in love is misdirected towards someone who cannot fulfil her demands on him, or, in fact, her. In Olivia's case, the action of the play involves a growth to self-awareness, and we can say that Olivia is very soon disabused of her affected mourning for her brother. However, she is then saddled by the action with an even worse situation, in that her healthy appetite for productive human contact has replaced her previous sterile attachment to mourning only to fix on a person who cannot reciprocate her feelings. So, she is made to suffer for a love which is not affected, just as Malvolio is made to suffer for his, which is clearly an affectation. Because he is only a steward, Malvolio is, almost by social definition, excluded from the world of eligible suitors for Olivia, except in his own mind.

Only the dramatic irony that Sebastian is alive, which no one in the play knows about (although the audience do) and that even Viola isn't sure of for most of the action, can solve Olivia's problem by offering her the possibility of fulfilment with a male object of her love. Sebastian is the key that will permit the various problems of Olivia, Orsino and Viola to be solved because, in effect, he squares the triangle. Shakespeare takes great care to introduce him at just the right moment, interrupting the action at the end of Act One. Olivia and Cesario have just met, Olivia has caught the plague of love and has sent Malvolio to give Cesario her ring, as clear a love token as it is possible to give. The act ends with Olivia committing her fortunes to fate just as Viola entrusts hers to time and we might next expect to see Malvolio catching up with Cesario. Instead, Sebastian enters and, unlike his sister, doesn't even ask where he is, and declares 'I am bound to the count Orsino's court farewell' (Shakespeare [1623] 2008: 2.1.38–9). This scene is structurally important because it comes between Olivia's realization that she is in love and Cesario being presented with the evidence of her love in the form of the ring. We are given a vital piece of information that, whilst maintaining our superior knowledge over the characters, gives us a clue as to how things will eventually come right, even before Viola knows they have gone wrong. It is both a strategic and a tactical move since in the long term it assures that everything will be well, but in the short term it opens the way for Shakespeare's exploitation of the discrepancy between Cesario's appearance and Viola's reality and of course it undercuts the tragic potential of Olivia having fallen in love with a girl disguised as a boy. Thus, to some extent, the tragic and painful aspects of Olivia's misapprehension are defused by our knowledge as experienced comic readers that, with each line that passes, Sebastian is getting nearer to Orsino's court. There is a lot of dramatic shorthand in action here, and we have to assume that Sebastian's appearance will untie the knot and that the brother can be a straightforward substitute for the sister and that if our sympathies have been enlisted for Olivia's unrequited passion, then we will want her to be married off. Even so, the whole business of substituting one twin for the other at the end of the play leaves too many questions open for it to be an entirely unchallenged satisfactory ending.

In fact, the play expends a very substantial amount of energy to make sure that the pain of Olivia's misdirected love is also contained by other aspects of its dynamic. The structure itself contains her painful interviews with Cesario by placing them in a context of scenes from the other plots. Thus, we find Olivia meeting Cesario in Act One Scene Five and we then meet Antonio and Sebastian with all that implies for the future of the plot, Malvolio and Cesario meet in Act Two Scene Three, a subplot scene of some length, Act Two Scene Four is devoted to Orsino and Cesario. The gulling of Malvolio in the box tree scene forms Act Two, Scene Five. Olivia's household, Cesario and Olivia come together in Act Three Scene One before giving way to an interview between Cesario and Olivia. Act Three Scene Two is a subplot scene and then Act Three Scene Three gives us Sebastian again, to undercut the tragic tendency of the interview between Olivia and Cesario, before Act Three Scene Four takes us back to Olivia's household and Malvolio's madness. Thus, in a typical piece of comic construction, we find that the tragic potential of events is undercut by its context, by the creation of what Coleridge would have called a comic wreath that works in two ways. First, by simply surrounding an important event with other events (we are perhaps all the heroes of our own tragedies and minor characters in other people's comedies) and secondly by the actual nature of those events. The subplot scenes that surround Olivia's hopeless love for Cesario are particularly concerned with the whole business of providing her with other suitors of various kinds. Sebastian, in our minds if not his, Malvolio, Orsino, Andrew and Cesario are all involved in this typical Shakespearean comedic approach of presenting aspects of the situation prismatically in each character's interaction with the others. All of these possible suitors to Olivia can be placed on a scale in terms of their self-awareness or self-deception and the extent to which they deceive others. This relates to the way that the action of the play concentrates so much on self-deception, affectation and self-indulgence. Olivia and Orsino are, in some ways, nearly as sick of self-love as Malvolio but he offers us a major example of overblown self-esteem and Shakespeare uses his amatory pretensions to provide comic perspective on the more serious love manoeuvrings of Olivia, Orsino and Cesario.

Of the three main self-deceivers, Orsino and Olivia in the end escape lightly, but Malvolio suffers to a greater degree, and this may be to some extent where some of the difficulties for the play as Romantic Comedy begin, because he cannot be assimilated into the comic syntheses. His attitude to Feste should show us that he is not intended to be a sympathetic character and he is self-deceived even before he sees the letter that acts as a catalyst to his ambitions. Apparently, he has been practising behaviour to his own shadow when he comes on in Act Two Scene Five, and he talks of precedents for becoming count Malvolio and for stewards marrying their mistresses even before he comes across the letter. He is in love with the idea of self-righteousness and hence the references to him as some kind of Puritan. He is not of course in any technical or religious sense a Puritan, but he does suffer from a besetting sin of theatrical Puritans, which is a conviction of his own rectitude and the essential worthlessness of others. But what happens to him is both more and less the comic revelation of his sins, since, although he is exposed as an object of ridicule, he is not brought face to face with his own ridiculousness. Malvolio is tormented by Toby and his fellows without any discernible amelioration in his behaviour and it is hard to see how he could be brought into the synthesis at the end, yet his very absence reveals just how partial that synthesis actually is. As is often the case, the characters in the subplot represent variations in less subtle form of what happened to the main characters and indeed Malvolio's presumption and Toby's idle mischief-making are to some extent a by-product of Olivia's obsession with mourning. Malvolio as steward oversees the decaying household and Toby is allowed a free hand precisely because Olivia is not around to check either of them. Ultimately the yellow-stockinged cross-gartered Malvolio is a visual physical enactment of the adoption of postures (disguises) to compare with the more rarefied actions of Orsino and Olivia in their willingness to act on temporary obsessions and to forget the necessity of observing true continuity in their lives. Just as Orsino pretends to be in love and Olivia to be in mourning so that they can hide from parts of themselves, so Malvolio's physical disguise is an attempt to hide the fact that he is a steward and therefore disqualified from being a suitable object of Olivia's affections. The physical means that he adopts to release him from his assigned role as steward are themselves a trap: he wears his garters and 'I could be sad. This does make some obstruction in the blood this cross gartering' (Shakespeare [1623] 2008: 3.4.19–20). The very means by which he hopes to achieve freedom causes constriction instead.

Why, then, would we feel any sympathy for Malvolio as he is persecuted for being a killjoy? Toby's defensive line in Act Two Scene Three is justly famous as a defence against Malvolio's failings: 'Dost thou think, because thou art virtuous, there shall be no more cakes and ale?' (Shakespeare [1623]

2008: 2.3.112–13). However, the problem lies to some extent with the people who are doing the persecuting and also with the fact that it is class-based, defending the status quo against the possibility of social mobility encapsulated in the idea of a steward marrying a lady. Andrew, Toby, Maria and the rather shadowy figure of Fabian are the main tormentors, but Feste plays only a minor part and ultimately helps as well as attacks Malvolio. The tormentors' world is one in which they too have their own problems in determining the limits of permissible behaviour since, even in the cakes and ale scene, Malvolio has some right on his side. In that scene, Maria appears with a warning 'If my lady has not called up her steward Malvolio and bid him turn you out of doors, never trust me' (Shakespeare [1623] 2008: 2.3.71–3). Malvolio's warning speech here includes the lines 'Is there no respect of place, persons, nor time in you?' (Shakespeare [1623] 2008: 2.3.89–90). In those words lies part of the answer to one of the play's central issues, because this is where the significance of the play's title comes in: Twelfth Night is the last day of the Christmas festivities, the end of a winter feast, a saturnalia when often the festivities involve some kind of suspension of the normal order in, for example, the election of a Lord of Misrule and so on.[2] It is a time of communal celebration and festivities held against the background of the harshness of the winter to come. The festivities are always touched by that knowledge, and the more so on the last evening of the feasts. The misrule of the feast was itself always conditioned by the fact that it was temporary, that it was a holiday and not reality, and we can discern this pattern operating in the structure of the play. Viola puts her trust in time to rectify the difficulties she finds herself in 'O time, thou must untangle this, not I./It is too hard a knot for me t'untie' (Shakespeare [1623] 2008: 2.2.40–1), but in the very next scene Toby proposes to destroy the natural progression of time by arguing that 'to go to bed after midnight is to go to bed betimes' (Shakespeare [1623] 2008: 2.3.8). Andrew may be stupid, but he knows that to be up late is to be up late, whereas Toby is trying to break down the natural order in favour of anarchy. In the same speech Toby asks if life doesn't consist of the four elements and Andrew replies that he thinks they're down to just eating and drinking. Malvolio is a threat to holiday, but his opposition in this scene depends on an understanding of the necessity of keeping an element of proportion. What ultimately happens to Malvolio is that his everyday disguise, his steward's clothes, is catastrophically exchanged for inappropriate holiday garb and it is entirely legitimate that those who defend the necessity of holiday and freedom from restraint should extract a revenge upon those who would deny it. The theme is familiar at least as far back as the *Bacchae* of Euripides. But in this case, the punishment for the man who cannot see the value of cakes and ale is that he is plagued with excess, a joke that begins to turn sour when we realize that Toby intends to 'carry it thus for our pleasure and his penance till our very pastime, tired out of breath, prompt us to have mercy on him' (Shakespeare [1623] 2008: 3.4.133–5). On the one hand, we have Toby who would extend holiday to encompass all existence, on the other we have Malvolio who would do away with it completely. But the play demonstrates that neither of these attitudes alone is enough.

In the case of *Twelfth Night* the question of disguise, the interchangeability of characters and the lack of perspicacity among the cast are foregrounded by the play itself, but some productions have also used questions around the construction of gender to considerable effect. At the Globe in 2002, Tim Carroll directed an all-male version of the play, notable for Mark Rylance playing Olivia (Figure 3). The somewhat spurious grounds for an all-male cast were that this was one of the Globe's original practice productions and therefore the female characters who would have been played by trained boys could be played by adult actors. Debates have long continued about the impact that these trained boys would have had without any definitive conclusions, but the fact that Rylance, who was forty-two years old in 2002, was playing a part that had originally probably been played by a young man in his teens or early twenties, rather undercuts arguments about authenticity.

Figure 3 Twelfth Night *by William Shakespeare, directed by Tim Carroll. Rhys Meredith (as Sebastian), Liam Brennan (as Orsino), Mark Rylance (as Olivia), Michael Brown (as Viola). Shakespeare's Globe Theatre, London, UK; 15 May 2002. Credit: Sheila Burnett/ ArenaPAL; www.arenapal.com*

This is not the place to examine the long controversy about authentic Renaissance playing in general or the Globe in particular, but clearly some practices may be more authentic than others.

Among the newspaper critics, Georgina Brown liked not only the authentic musical instruments but also the all-male cast: 'the effect in this most charming, funny, sexy and subtle of all Shakespeare's comedies of errors is to underline our human reliance on disguise and play acting, especially when it comes to affairs of the heart' (*Mail on Sunday*: 2 June 2002). Similarly, Nicholas de Jongh thought the play was ripe for such a treatment:

It was high time this most sexually ambiguous of all Shakespeare's plays enjoyed the services of an all-male cast. Tim Carroll's thoughtful Elizabethan production duly obliges and begins to cast a fresh light upon the tragicomedy. 'Begins' is the operative word. For although Carroll honourably rejects crude drag-appeal or the pantomimic tendency that's sometimes prevalent at this address, his Twelfth Night slightly lacks the courage of its cross-dressing. It's as though there was fear of the comedy's bisexual slanting. Nevertheless, his production vividly reflects Shakespeare's sense of the fluidity and arbitrary drive of an erotic desire that leaps the bounds of gender.

(*Evening Standard*: 23 May 2002)

At the National Theatre in 2017 director Simon Godwin focused on the character of Malvolio, presenting a regendered Malvolia, played by Tamsin Greig, as 'a social climber who's the sworn enemy of frivolity. In this gender-bending take on a play that's already fixated with muddles over identity, he's reimagined as Malvolia, a prim fantasist with a taste for starchy outfits and a startlingly severe helmet of jet-black hair' (Henry Hitchings, *Evening Standard*: 23 February). John Nathan shrugged over 'the latest recent example of a major production switching the gender of a traditionally male Shakespearean character, a thing now so established it's hardly worth mentioning, especially in a play whose barmy plot pivots on a female pretending to be male' (*Jewish Chronicle*: 3 March). Paul Taylor, however, pointed out a very significant difference:

Tamsin Greig joins the ranks of the great actresses who are now tackling major Shakespearean roles – Glenda Jackson as Lear; Harriet Walter as Brutus, Henry IV, and Prospero; Michelle Terry as Henry V. The difference is that whereas they played these characters as men, there's been a gender re-think for Greig's funny and ultimately desolating portrayal of this repressive Puritan. The legislation that made same-sex marriages possible has also rendered a female version of the character feasible.

(Paul Taylor, *Independent*: 24 February)

The production also suggested that Andrew and Toby might have had a sexual relationship in the past and that Antonio had something of a crush on Sebastian, exacerbated by the fact that the Elephant Inn where they lodge has metamorphosed into what Michael Billington called 'a gay-hotel-cum-disco' (*The Guardian*: 23 February) complete with a drag queen singing interpolated Shakespearian melodies including Hamlet's 'To be or not to be'. As Christopher Hart pointed out (*Sunday Times*: 26 February), the production was accompanied by programme notes that underlined the message: '"Is the play suggesting that gender and sex are as much social constructs as physical ones?" And it tuts disapprovingly—one might even say puritanically – over what it calls Twelfth Night's "somewhat heteronormative conclusion".'

Traditional Romantic Comedies will tend to have 'somewhat heteronormative' conclusions because heterosexual (married) couples have been virtually the only sanctioned groupings permitted by both stage actions and extra-theatrical social structures until very recently. Only when conventions change both in society and in the theatre does it become possible to begin to search out latent possibilities and to explore non-heteronormative elements within what appear on the surface to be examples of the truism that (heterosexual) love and marriage go together like a horse and carriage and you can't have one without the other.

Orsino's last words are of his fancy, a word which itself picks up the end of his first speech in the play and could make us uneasy about the changes which are supposed to have happened to him. Not only that, but the stage picture is unbalanced. Traditionally we ought to have two couples each made up of a man and a woman, but we actually have three people in male dress which visually undercuts the expected comic pattern of the final scene. After that, the stage is left empty for the professional jester, the only person apart from Viola who has moved easily from household to household and who has shared with her insights into the workings of Illyria, who has partaken of all the worlds of the play, but who now belongs to none of them. The concluding song is of nature and natural cycles, perhaps a reminder of how the pervasive influence of nature in the *Dream* has shrunk here and how there is no green space to act as a corrective to the manners of the court unless you think of Illyria itself as being that corrective. Ultimately though, *Twelfth Night* appears to give up much of the ground that Shakespeare had won in comedies such as *A Midsummer Night's Dream* and *As You Like It* and contains within itself a questioning of the comic pattern that contains the potential for its own destruction.

2

Romantic Comedy:
1660–1895

Contexts

It is perhaps paradoxical that a specifically Shakespearian Romantic Comedy should not be the dominant type of Romantic Comedy to be written and staged in the period from 1660 to the twentieth century. Instead, the significant type of new comic writing that dominates our interest in the period owed much to the developments of a form derived from Ben Jonson (1572–1637), whose Comedy of Humours was a major influence on a developing a Comedy of Manners that would dominate English Romantic Comedy for over two centuries. Stanley Cavell argues with some justification that 'Shakespearean romantic comedy did not remain a viable form of comedy for the English stage, compared with a Jonsonian comedy of manners' (Cavell 1981: 19), although that is to ignore the very important fact that Shakespeare's comedies themselves can easily be regarded as filling that theatrical role in their own right, since many of the comedies were staged very successfully throughout the period from 1600 to 1900 and beyond. Cavell also quotes Northrop Frye's argument that '[a]ll the important writers of English comedy since Jonson have cultivated the comedy of manners with its realistic illusion and not Shakespeare's romantic and stylized kind'

(Cavell 1981: 51). Although modern critics and productions concentrate on the livelier examples of comedic drama from this period, for a considerable time many of the writers whose work we now value found themselves battling against the pervasive influence of what came to be called Sentimental Comedy that exerted a powerful negative power over the theatrical practice of the period.

Shakespeare's last plays, dating from the early years of the second decade of the seventeenth century, have enough characteristics in common to have attracted the label Romances, that label, however, stresses not so much relationships between young lovers as the plays' tendency to concentrate on other aspects of Romance in their use of epic narratives, sea voyages, improbable plots, miraculous discoveries, amazing coincidences and recognition of long-lost characters through preserved tokens that identify who they really are. However, there were major social, political and theatrical changes that meant the period after 1660 was radically different from that when Shakespeare's last plays were first staged. During the reign of King Charles I (1600–49) a growing struggle between the king and parliament had resulted from political tensions between the two that blew up into a full-scale civil war between the forces of parliament and the king. Charles I was defeated and held in captivity until he was executed in 1649 and a republic under the parliamentary leader Oliver Cromwell was declared. The unprecedented judicial killing of a king ran alongside a ferment of new political ideas that helped to change the intellectual climate. Charles II, son of Charles I, was forced to flee into exile in continental Europe and the period of Cromwell's rule was characterized by considerable political and intellectual debate. During this interregnum and under the influence of political ideas about the sinfulness of the theatre, the theatres were closed from 1642 and only a very few clandestine performances took place in this period. After Cromwell died in 1658, and a not very successful period under his son Richard, parliament decided to recall the exiled Charles II to take over as king again in 1660 (The Restoration).

The impact of the changes during the interregnum was profound in that it altered the relationship between crown and parliament forever and fundamentally shook the foundations on which the social contract between the government and the ruled was based. The Restoration to the throne of Charles II in 1660, eleven years after his father, Charles I, had been executed, was also accompanied by significant innovations in British theatrical practice. During their exiles in continental Europe Charles and his followers were subject to many influences that would be brought back into the English court at his Restoration. The theatres had been officially closed for over a decade and their reopening was an occasion for many changes. The introduction of actresses to play women's parts helped to alter the ways in which women were portrayed on stage, the extended use of changeable scenery, and the effective final replacement of the old outdoor amphitheatres with smaller indoor theatres also contributed significantly to creating the theatrical climate of the times. Outside the theatre, philosophy and creative writing were very influenced by a tendency to scientific enquiry that privileged the apparent precision of prose over the allusiveness of poetry. Although verse continued to be a significant factor in the writing of new tragedy for some time, comedies were now routinely written in prose.

The Country Wife and *The Way of the World*

English comedies from the Restoration period and similar works such as *She Stoops to Conquer* (1773), in which the social conventions and customs of a leisured class sustain the dramatic impetus are often described as Comedies of Manners. Such comedies are often defined in terms that suggest a superficial concern with fashions, decorum and etiquette, but their starting point is the view that human behaviour, including romantic behaviour, is patterned and consists of systems of codes and conventions (often implicit rather than explicit) that impose an order on experience by making it predictable and manageable. Romantic love poses a significant challenge to the good ordering of a society by testing the rules of the social order against the demands of the individual. Comedies of Manners may test the limits of social codes and reveal their arbitrariness often through testing the limits of what is romantically viable, but they normally end with the restoration of order through, as in *She Stoops*, multiple betrothals or marriages that channel potentially anarchic energies into socially acceptable forms. Comedies of Manners often scrutinize the values enshrined in a social code, comparing and contrasting them with those that people actually live by, particularly in terms of sexual relations. Comedy in the later years of the seventeenth century was characterized by such an approach, ultimately derived from Ben Jonson's Comedy of Humours in which characters were deemed to be representative of a prevailing disposition towards certain kinds of behaviour. This stemmed from which of the four humours (bodily fluids) prevailed in a person's constitution: if blood predominated, you were sanguine, phlegm made you phlegmatic, yellow bile made you angry (choleric) and black bile led to melancholy. If all the fluids were well balanced, so too would you be. Characters' names could easily be made to serve as in index to their humours and thus to their underlying dispositions.

This Jonsonian emphasis helped to create a broadly satirical comedy in the Restoration period, in which fashionable society was reflected to itself in plays that explored the sexual behaviour, social customs and conventions of a narrow group of aristocrats, landowners, the rich and their families as they attempted to negotiate the intricacies of the new social order. Although there would be some changes in the status of women of the landed classes during the period from the Restoration to the death of Queen Victoria, neither society nor the theatre broke out entirely from the pattern that was aptly delineated in such works as William Wycherley's *The Country Wife* (1667) or George Etherege's *The Man of Mode* (1676). The prevailing attitude towards romance and marriage throughout the later seventeenth, eighteenth and nineteenth centuries is one heavily influenced by what the poet Samuel Butler saw as the mercenary nature of marriage:

> For Matrimony's but a bargain made
> To serve the turns of interest and of trade;
> Not out of love or kindness, but designs,
> To settle land and tenements like fines.
>
> (Quoted in Dabhoiwala 2012: 202)

In *The Country Wife* the Romantic Comedy elements are confined to the plot in which Frank Harcourt attempts to persuade Alithea to marry him, while the surrounding action centres on the efforts of Horner to have sex with as many women as possible, including the eponymous Country Wife. Similarly in *The Man of Mode* the main interest is in tracing the adventures of a rake, Dorimant, who finally succumbs to the realization that the only way to have sex with his beloved Harriet is to marry her. By 1700, after the deposition of the catholic James II, Charles II's brother, as king in favour of the protestant William and Mary, although the contours of the dramatic landscape are not unfamiliar, the dramatists' viewpoint has changed and we find ourselves viewing the territory from a slightly different perspective in William Congreve's *The Way of the World* (1700). Far-reaching political changes and developments in social and ethical attitudes separate the two periods and comedy in this play has moved away from the more purely satirical Jonsonian approach towards a world view that has room for elements of generosity towards others. Congreve's vision of the world is less nihilistic than either Wycherley's or Etherege's and there is an important stress on the need for reconciliation that we can exemplify from the different way that the Wycherley and Congreve approach the concluding dances in their plays. In *The Country Wife* there is a dance of cuckolds to celebrate Horner's triumphs; in *The Way of the World* the dance is a dance of reconciliation that appears to involve many of the leading characters.

Although we are still recognizably in the same kind of territory covered by the earlier plays, most of the characters in *The Way of the World* have some redeeming feature. Moreover, the action of the play is not concerned centrally with cuckolding but rather with the question of who will get to marry Millamant in a simple 'heroine threatened by the power of a relative' plot. Congreve himself tells us that his methods are different from those of traditional (Jonsonian) comedy when he says in the dedication to the play that '[t]hose characters which are meant to be ridiculous in most of our comedies are of fools so gross that, in my humble opinion, they should rather disturb than divert the well-natured and reflecting part of an audience; they are rather objects of charity than contempt; and instead of moving our mirth, they ought very often to excite our compassion'. So here we have Congreve stressing compassion charity and reflection as significant parts of how an audience should react to natural fools. He goes on: 'This reflection moved me to design some characters which should appear ridiculous not so much through a natural folly (which is incorrigible, and therefore not proper for the stage) as through an affected wit' (Congreve [1700] in Griffiths and Trussler 2005: 246–7). In plays such as *The Country Wife* characters like Horner also despise affectation but Congreve's is a world with a gentler approach, perhaps qualified as a result of Jeremy Collier's 1698 attacks on the stage in his *Short View of the Immorality and Profaneness of the English Stage* and by the growing tendency towards Sentimentalism. Although the factors associated with rise of Sentimentalism are complex and the term itself has somewhat fallen out of favour in theatrical scholarship (Hume 1977: 249), *The Way of the World* remains very much centred on Sentimentalism's preoccupation with the question of right and wrong ways of behaving, particularly as they determine the appropriateness or otherwise of particular social pairings. Although the names of the characters do certainly carry meaning in the Jonsonian humours tradition, they do not define their characters as closely as is the case in, for example, *The Country Wife*. Broadly speaking, the impulse towards Sentimentalism, a philosophical position associated with the third Lord Shaftesbury (1671–1713) in opposition to the more radically negative theories of Thomas Hobbes (1588–1679), was the idea that Nature was essentially benevolent, and that 'virtue is centred in a natural impulse towards humanitarian feeling for and sympathy with one's fellows' while 'the exercise of this virtue is accompanied by an inward feeling of satisfaction and joy, while the spectacle of distress produces sympathetic pain' (Tuveson 1953: 268). Such views were influential and their opposition towards the supposed satirical excesses of Restoration comedy, produced some dire eighteenth-century comedies that have not survived in the repertory, but they also cast a long shadow in the theatre over such works as Goldsmith's *She Stoops to Conquer*.

The Way of The World has a very complex plot that can be quite difficult to follow in any detail, particularly in the theatre and it almost seems to revel in that complexity of inter-relationships, obligations, pretences and secret alliances. For the audience, as for the characters, the challenge is to follow the trail, pick up the meaning of the clues and work out the underlying pattern of emotional connections and how that relates to the various legal and familial realities. It is no accident that in the play itself, early in Act One, Congreve appears to signal his own enjoyment of the complexity of the relationships that he has created when, reducing sacred aristocratic genealogical trees to meaningless nonsense, he has Fainall describe Sir Wilfull to Mirabell: '[H]e is half-brother to this Witwoud by a former wife, who was sister to my Lady Wishfort, my wife's mother. If you marry Millamant you must call cousins too' (Congreve [1700] in Griffiths and Trussler 2005: 258). If the family relationships are tangled, so are the emotional ties that link characters. In the first edition of the play, the cast list is glossed with explanatory epithets that delineate the formal and emotional complexities both within and outside family groups. Characters are described as 'in love with' other characters, others are friends or former friends or described as loving or liking Mirabell. So, the existing social obligations of the characters in *The Way of the World* are presented through the complexities of both familial ties and the legal bonds associated with marriage. Petulant, Mrs Marwood and the servants appear to be the only characters apart from Mirabell who are not already in some kind of actual family relationship with one another. The action of the play is concerned with unmasking the underlying realities and trying to bring the surface patterns into a closer relationship with those underlying realities.

Generally, our attitudes to the major characters in any play are likely to be more complex than those towards more minor characters, so I think the point about the complexity of characterization can be best demonstrated in the more peripheral figures of Marwood and Wilfull Witwoud. Wilfull Witwoud is very much the same kind of figure as Sparkish in *The Country Wife*, as his surname suggests, yet Marwood, whose name indicates her status as a would-be wrecker, is the only person who is not extremely rude to Wilfull when he arrives in his muddy boots, and Wilfull, despite appearing coarse and insensitive in his wooing of Millamant, is the only person quick enough to be able to attempt to defend Mrs Fainall from her husband's drawn sword. Similarly, we can compare Wilfull's rejection of Millamant instructively with Sparkish's of Alethea in *The Country Wife*. Wilfull says 'S'heart, aunt, I have no mind to marry. My cousin's a fine lady, and the gentleman loves her and she loves him, and they deserve one another' (Congreve [1700] in Griffiths and Trussler 2005: 346). Contrast this with Sparkish in the earlier play. He says 'I never had any passion for you till now – for now I hate you. 'Tis true I might have married your portion ... I'll come to your wedding and resign you with as much joy as I would a stale wench to a new cully; nay with as much joy as I would after the first night, if I had been married to you' (Wycherley [1675] in Griffiths and Trussler 2005: 136). The later play manifests a much more tolerant, benevolent and unembittered view than the earlier one. Wilfull is a country bumpkin, and his half-brother Tony is a town fop but in terms of the action of the play the fact that they are related to most of the central characters can seem almost unnecessarily complicated. Although this set of relationships creates a picture of an enclosed world that it is almost impossible to escape because almost no-one is outside the pattern, audience attempts to understand the patterning can be confusing, particularly in the earlier scenes of the play. In 2018 the director James Macdonald chose to cast a black actor Fisayo Akinade as Witwoud while his half-brother Sir Witwoud was the white actor Christian Patterson. In the same production Mrs Marwood (Jenny Jules) and Petulant (Simon Manyonda) were also played by black actors as were several, but not all, the servants. No attempt was made to explain the casting and it attracted no critical notice. In this case, it appears that this example of a more inclusive approach to casting made no significant impact on the audience.

At times, the action of *The Way of the World* resembles a kaleidoscopic card game in which successive players attempt to trump the last player's bid. It begins with Mirabell and Fainall getting up from cards, so that they are presented from the opening of the action as in some kind of contest with one another. Despite Mirabell using the name Fainall in the very first line of the play (a name that might literally suggest what we should think about him) it is by no means clear in this early scene which of these apparent friends will turn out to be the hero and which the villain. Moreover, it seems that the plot springs from a competitive legacy hunt in which Mirabell is saved from potential accusations of being entirely mercenary only by the general sense that he and Millamant are mutually suited to each other. Lady Wishfort controls half the fortune of Millamant and apparently also has legal power over Mrs Fainall's wealth, so that Fainall and Mirabell are in conflict over controlling significant sums of money, as each of them tries to get Lady Wishfort to make a disposition in their own favour. Each uses a series of stratagems designed to destabilize her social position and make her dependent on one or other of them. However, it is worth noting that, as so often in Romantic Comedy, the actual monetary sums involved are considerably beyond what would be necessary to sustain a very good lifestyle in the real world. Millamant already controls half her fortune, a sum (£3,000) that would be sufficient to maintain an extremely high standard of living, but she chooses to regard obtaining the other half from Lady Wishfort as a necessity before she will agree to marry. She turns the men's legacy hunt into a kind of chivalric contest in which Mirabell has to pass her tests before he is deemed fit to marry her.

The play operates by trying to match ideals of moral conduct with the realities of social experience through a more complete and reconciliatory morality than in the earlier plays of the immediate post-Restoration period. While the social obligations of the characters in this world are presented through the medium of the law and also through an extremely complicated set of family relationships, the situation is based very much on Congreve's desire to bring the outward expression of human relationships, such as marriages and legal documents, to match the inward states of human emotions. In the context of any discrepancy between appearance and reality, then a character who is aware of that discrepancy is in a position of power over others. This is the whole basis of Horner's strategy in *The Country Wife*, and at the beginning of *The Way of the World* Congreve has Mirabell trying to set up a similar situation by tricking Lady Wishfort into apparently marrying his servant Waitwell and then extricating her from the embarrassment in return for being able to marry Millamant with all her wealth. Here perhaps is the clearest difference between the earlier plays and *The Way of the World*, since in the earlier plays the split between appearances and realities is investigated but seen ultimately as being useful to the characters, perhaps even desirable, whilst in *The Way of the World* the truth emerges and there is a sense of cleansing as outward appearance and inner reality finally match.

Throughout the play Congreve reveals his own hand very gradually. Much of the apparent complexity and certainly much of the verisimilitude of the play can be seen as deriving from the gradual revelation of the facts that underpin the various facades of Mirabell's relationship with Mrs Fainall, Fainall's relationship with Marwood and Marwood's relationship with Fainall. Complexity develops as each secret is revealed, and that complexity is enhanced by the way that the initially unknown relationships each refer inside the already-established group of characters, so that there appears to be no way out for the characters within the tightly knit world of the play. The family tree is complicated, but the pattern of emotional ties is even more so, since the family relationships are fixed by permanent events like birth, while the emotional tangle is still capable of being developed. There is a large discrepancy between the family structures sanctioned by legal convention and the emotional structures that stand in the way of Mirabell and Millamant marrying. The complexity of the plot and the pattern of hidden connections between the characters means that the action of the play is both a contest between different readings of 'the way of the world' and a test of the values represented by the concepts of family and emotion.

The structure of the play is itself a positive factor in the treatment of the contrasts between reality and appearances. In each act, family relationships and emotional relationships are tested to see which has greater validity. As one would expect, Act One deals very much with the revelation of the outward conventions of the society that the play is concerned with: family relationships, open loves like Mirabell's for Millamant, and socially sanctioned friendships. However, there are clear hints, insinuations, and evasions that reveal the underlying fluidity and uncertainty of the true emotional situation that bedevils the romantic hero and heroine in their struggle to achieve the goal of marriage. Act One tells us that Mirabell really loves Millamant but has pretended to love Lady Wishfort, and this plot has been revealed by Marwood, whilst Act Two reveals that Marwood is in love with Mirabell (which is why she denounced his plots to Lady Wishfort) but is also the current mistress of Fainall, whose wife (the daughter of Lady Wishfort) is the former mistress and current confidant of Mirabell.

Act Two reveals the underlying emotional situation and
throughout the play the crosscurrents of the emotional
situation emerge more openly and assume greater importance.
This is quite logical since the family relationships are largely
fixed by reasons of birth and marriage and are therefore less
readily susceptible to change. In Act Two, these emotional
undercurrents began to be revealed to the audience, if not to
the other characters, as we come to grasp the complexities of
the situation involving the Fainalls, Mirabell and Marwood.
This is achieved in part by a structural juxtaposition of scenes
between a husband and his mistress (Fainall and Marwood)
and between a lover and his ex-mistress (Mirabell and Mrs
Fainall) in which the ex-mistress is the wife of the husband. In
this act the action moves from the bitterness of the adulterous
couple, Fainall and Marwood, through the forgiving couple
of ex-lovers, Mirabell and Mrs Fainall, to the meeting of the
pair who represent the play's ideal romantic couple, Mirabell
and Millamant. This type of construction is typical of the
play: each act tends to have an almost formal progression
of incidents and characters displaying aspects of the theme,
possibly deriving from the approach of French classical drama.

To some extent Act Three is taken up with the establishment
of new characters and with other characters beginning to
learn some of the information revealed to us in the previous
act. Marwood's role becomes increasingly significant in Act
Three because her desire to do something about the emotional
realities assumes crucial importance in the development of the
plot when she learns of Mirabell's new scheme with Waitwell
and his previous involvement with Mrs Fainall. She is not
related to any of the leading characters in any legal sense, but
only by her various emotional commitments. Those emotional
ties are much more significant than the family ties that bring
Wilfull to London. As the act progresses, the family ties
that bulked so large in Act One are revealed as increasingly
unimportant compared to the emotional bonds. Crucially
Marwood overhears the plot to marry off Waitwell and Foible
(Lady Wishfort's maid) before Waitwell woos Lady Wishfort

in the guise of Sir Rowland. This subterfuge is part of a stratagem whereby Mirabell is hoping able to exert power over Lady Wishfort when she discovers that she has inadvertently married his servant.

In Act Four, the interest is centred on marriage and the ways in which it can manifest social or emotional reality. The key encounter is between Mirabell and Millamant in the so-called 'proviso' scene, but the action is structured around a succession of proposals of marriage mainly to Millamant but also to Lady Wishfort by Waitwell, in his disguise as Sir Rowland. The first courtship scene involves Wilfull, the boorish countryman courting Millamant not out of love but duty and for dynastic reasons, unable to match Millamant's sophisticated wit with his uneducated country manners. He is brought back by Lady Wishfort after Petulant's brief outburst, 'Look you, Mrs Millamant, if you can love me, dear nymph say it – and that's the conclusion – pass on, or pass off – that's all' (Congreve [1700] in Griffiths and Trussler 2005: 320). In contrast to the perfunctory proposals of Wilfull and Petulant, the courtship scene between Millamant and Mirabell represents the fullest working out within the play of how to conduct the business of marriage. The declarations of love are presented through the same external social patterns as predominate in the rest of play: the language is the language of legal business and the formal qualities of the debate suggest a process of examination and cross-examination. The important factor is that the ground should be cleared between Mirabell and Millamant for a mutual understanding that can form the basis for a true marriage of two minds. As they co-operate to reach agreement, we see how it is possible for social forms to be made to match an emotional reality and how Mirabell and Millamant can arrive at an understanding of each other that will lead to a marriage of true free spirits.

Before this scene Millamant, as her name perhaps suggests, adopts a light-hearted approach to love, but here she deals with aspects of the social patterns of marriage insisting that marriage should not be allowed to alter her way of life totally, that she can maintain her own personality, that the two of them will not indulge in excessive behaviour in public, and that she can continue to have friends without Mirabell being jealous. These provisos are all presented in a whimsical way but Mirabell's are presented in a more judicial fashion. This is particularly noticeable in the case of Mirabell's specifically sexual provisos where the judicial language appears to help to make them more acceptable to Millamant. By the end of the scene they have agreed on a pattern which seems viable to them and it is significant that each sees the ideal of marriage in organic rather than mechanical terms: Millamant says 'I may by degrees dwindle into a wife' and Mirabell replies that he wishes to impose conditions so that 'when you are dwindled into a wife, I may not be beyond measure enlarged into a husband' (Congreve [1700] in Griffiths and Trussler 2005: 316–17). This is in marked contrast to the more normal disjunction between the roles of lover and spouse in the play which is dramatized in the marital relationships of the Fainalls, in lines like his rhetorical question to Marwood, 'could you think, because the nodding husband would not wake, that e'er the watchful lover slept?' (Congreve [1700] in Griffiths and Trussler 2005: 274). Fainall sees the roles of lover and husband as necessarily divorced from one another: the real emotion associated with love is not the same as the external appearances of being a husband. However, Mirabell sees himself growing into a husband with a harmony between the outward form and the reality: he wants to marry the woman he loves and unite the emotional and legal states.

Romantic rhetoric is not in great supply in Act Four until the final marriage proposal of the act. Although the vocabulary of romance makes an appearance as Waitwell makes his move, it is top heavy with its own fraudulence: 'My impatience, madam, is the effect of my transport; and till I have the possession of your adorable person, I am tantalized on a rack, and do but hang, madam, on the tenter of expectation.' Lady Wishfort's reply 'You have excess of gallantry' (Congreve [1700] in Griffiths and Trussler 2005: 324) is a reminder that serves to confirm the audience in its conviction that Waitwell is a false and sentimental lover, even if he is working in Mirabell's cause. The excessive vocabulary of supposed true emotion is revealed as hollow and pretentious and the scene between Mirabell and Millamant stands out in even sharper focus as representing the best and most viable approach to human relationships within the play. The sequence of proposals here is largely coloured by excessive abruptness, excessive drunkenness or excessive gallantry, so that the formal balance of the alternating conditions of Millamant and Mirabell is put into even sharper and more desirable focus. Around them, we see the conventional unhappy marriage of the Fainalls and the affectations of all the other suitors, stressing again the importance of self-discipline and mutual respect in the creation of a happy marriage. In terms of the story of Millamant and Mirabell, all that remains in Act Five is to remove the external barriers to the uniting of their internal and external states. So, when the play turns into a series of revelations and counter revelations in Act Five, Lady Wishfort gets to the truth of her encounter with Waitwell, Marwood reveals Mrs Fainall's former affair with Mirabell and Fainall threatens to denounce them all to the waiting world. Each of these revelations represents attempts from different standpoints to match up the emotional and social structures with one another. In Act Five, emotion seems to be in complete control in the shape of Marwood and Fainall, as they attempt to manipulate the family relationships – and thereby control over the wealth – in favour of their own emotional realities. Fainall's attempted blackmail of Lady Wishfort is interestingly not thwarted by the revelation of his affair with Marwood as one might expect, precisely because he is not operating by quite the same set of values as the others. He appears happy to accept the disjunction between the social order and the emotional order, and he believes that his prize for not revealing that disjunction should be an increase in his material possessions, thus making the gap between social order and emotional facts even greater. Wilfull may draw his sword in defence of family values but ultimately it is Mirabell's deed which is the means to bring emotional and family relationships into the desired balance. Fainall's defeat will ultimately be at the hands of Mirabell, the man who has the best knowledge of the gap between the apparent situation and the real situation. Mirabell produces the deed of trusteeship which negates Fainall's plans, so by the end of the play the family emotional realities are finally bought into an appropriate equilibrium or even fused.

This happens with the final revelations where once again the pattern is that the person who knows the difference between the visible and hidden facts appears to have a power of others which is then ended by the revelation of further hidden facts. While this is most obviously for true for Fainall and Mirabell, we can apply much the same terms to the development of the relationship between Mirabell and Millamant where she has power over Mirabell because he is known to love her, while she has concealed her own feelings until the proviso scene. However, although we have been privy to many of the facts unknown to the characters, we have not been aware of the final stratagem, the trump card that saves Mrs Fainall from her husband, in the appearance of the trust deed that gives Mirabell power over Mrs Fainall's fortune.

The triumph of Mirabell suggests that the true reality is the internal bonds of emotional commitment, a changing and fluid reality which should generate the outward pattern of overt social relationships. When for some reason the inner and outer realities do not correspond, a situation of ironic power arises in which anyone who knows the underlying facts has power over those who do not. This is a familiar pattern in comedy. The solution to the problems posed by the imbalance is to create a social framework that actually reflects the true internal emotional situation, and this is achieved in *The Way of the World* by the revelation of the underlying emotional order and then the creation of a new social order to reflect that emotional order. At an ideological level, Romantic Comedy works to suggest that there is an emotional order that offers an achievable rightness in the domain of feeling. While at one level the trust deed produced by Mirabell at the end of the play is no more than the simple dramatist's device to cut through an impossibly complex situation, a Deus Ex Machina imposing a new order from outside, it is also much more. It is not only the final hidden secret at the bottom of the pattern of revelations about the hidden emotional structures, but also a fundamental basis on which the new social order may be built because through it all the characters who appear to depend on Lady Wishfort are finally emancipated. Millamant gets her freedom and her money because of this revelation, Mrs Fainall is shown to be not dependant on Lady Wishfort, Wilfull no longer has to pay suit to Millamant, and even Witwoud and Petulant appear to have broken free from Lady Wishfort. So in general terms we can see the play as a double action, testing emotional realities against social realities, gradually revealing the discrepancy between underlying emotional realities and outer social forms, and, equally gradually, attempting to create a new social order to reflect the disposition of emotional commitments.

Even the way that this world cannot accommodate Marwood in the new order and can only hope that Fainall will come round suggest that this is more than a routine comedy. It is not just a comedy of surface manners because it asks what lies underneath the social forms and how they are generated. In many ways it is a triumph, but it also is the end of an era. It is Congreve's last play and deals with affirmation and reconciliation as much as with sceptical satire. Its hero is after all meant to be admirable and there is a kind of blurring of sexual roles in the names Mirabell and Millamant that points towards the eighteenth-century development of a genteel sentimental comedy. Millamant herself accuses Mirabell of being sententious, that is of talking in moral maxims and he is given to talking about having children to his future wife that suggests quite a quite fundamental change from some of the earlier works in the Restoration tradition. Satire is giving way to affirmation and the balance that we find between the two forms within one comedy in this play gave way to the eighteenth century's so-called sentimental comedy of Sir

Richard Steele and other less talented purveyors of sentiment and sententiousness.

A Bold Stroke for a Wife

Susanna Centlivre (probably 1669–1723) was one of the relatively few women writers who succeeded as theatrical authors in the early eighteenth century.[1] She was, inevitably, lauded as a successor to Aphra Behn (1640–89) and some of her plays stayed in the repertory until the end of the nineteenth century. Like most of her contemporaries, particularly the women writers, her works are now seldom staged, although some could be effectively revived today. As a woman writer, Centlivre was an easy target for the partisans of sentimentality who attacked her and her works in a variety of familiar ways: sensational biographies that luxuriated in her supposed sexual escapades were matched by attacks on the broadness of her topics and her treatment of them. *A Bold Stroke for a Wife* (1718), however, offers some interesting variations on themes drawn from the stock-in-trade of Romantic Comedy. The situation is a variation on a familiar motif: Anne Lovely is a rich heiress whose father has died, leaving her in the charge of four guardians who all have to agree before she can be married and retain possession of her (enormous) fortune of £30,000. Her father has vindictively chosen her guardians so that the chance of them agreeing about the merits of any suitor is extremely low. At the beginning of the play Anne has already met Colonel Fainwell and fallen in love with him. Unlike Congreve's negatively judged Fainall, this Fainwell will have to dissemble well in order to win his bride. There is no other plot involving other potential suitors or a second potential bride, leaving the stage clear for the hero to find a way to be allowed to marry his beloved. Fainwell's task is to find ways of gaining all four guardians' permission for him to marry Anne. Her dead father has tried to warp the future behaviour of his daughter by imposing the dead hand of patriarchal prohibition on her actions. Unlike Portia's father in *The Merchant of Venice*, Anne's father's constraints on her behaviour are not aimed at helping her to an appropriate choice of partner, but at frustrating any possibility of her being able to marry at all. According to Sackbut, an innkeeper who had been the father's servant: 'He hated posterity, you must know, and wished the world were to expire with himself' (Centlivre [1718] 1995: 54). Failing that possibility, he had arranged the four incompatible guardians whom Anne could never hope to please. Thus the negative aspects of patriarchal power are diffused among the very whimsical characters who control Anne's destiny: Sir Philip Modelove, described in the Dramatis Personae as 'an old beau'; Periwinkle, 'a silly virtuoso' (which means he collects antiquarian oddities and strange examples of flora and fauna); Tradelove, 'a changebroker' (stock market speculator); and Obadiah Prim, 'a Quaker' (Centlivre [1718] 1995: 49). Fainwell must find ways to neutralize the guardians' power by persuading each of them to agree to him marrying Anne, which he does by adopting a series of disguises in which he plays upon their idiosyncrasies and eventually manages the apparently impossible task of getting all four to agree by 'feigning well'. Centlivre use the opportunities offered by the four guardians to satirize contemporary morals and manners as well as advancing the plot. The targets are fairly obvious: the gullibility of the aging beau, besotted by appearances, of the virtuoso ever seeking a novelty curio, and of the speculator forever looking for a good deal which will make his fortune are familiar from many Comedies of Manners, as are the names that point us to their dominant humours. So, too, is Prim, the religious hypocrite, who blames Anne's low-cut dress for stirring up his own lust and insists on her changing out of her finery into a Quaker dress, a move that finds a later and more significant parallel in *She Stoops to Conquer*.

In the early scenes of *A Bold Stroke for a Wife*, Centlivre overtly stresses the resemblances between the predicament Fainwell and Anne find themselves in and a heroic quest fairy tale in which the hero must perform a series of apparently impossible tasks in order to win the heroine. Freeman, Fainwell's friend, states that 'if it depended upon knight-errantry, I should not doubt your setting free the damsel' (Centlivre [1718] 1995: 56) and Betty, Anne's maid and confidante, echoes him: 'Well! I have read of enchanted castles, ladies delivered from the chains of magic, giants killed, and monsters overcome; so that I shall be the less surprized if the Colonel should conjure you out of the power of your guardians' (Centlivre [1718] 1995: 61). Similarly both Fainwell and Anne see their difficulties in terms of classical exemplars and the great tradition of love. Fainwell ends Act One Scene One: 'The path of love's a dark and dangerous way, / Without a landmark, or one friendly star, /And he that runs the risk, deserves the fair' (Centlivre [1718] 1995: 59). Anne ends Act One Scene Two thus: 'Oh all ye powers that favor happy lovers, grant he may be mine! Thou god of love, if you be'st ought but name, assist my Fainwell. /Point all thy darts to aid my love's design, /And make his plots as prevalent as thine' (Centlivre [1718] 1995: 61). Despite the best efforts of the guardians to thwart the marriage, their own failings eventually ensure that the colonel and the woman are able to marry: convention and hypocrisy are forced into flight by the hero successfully storming the defences put up around the heroine and we can only assume that they live happily ever after.

She Stoops to Conquer

By the time Oliver Goldsmith wrote *She Stoops to Conquer* in the 1770s the sentimentalism that is parodied in Congreve's presentation of Sir Rowland in *The Way of The World* and Centlivre's presentation of the Quaker guardian had come to dominate both thinking about comedy and the nature of comic performance. Goldsmith found it necessary to prepare the ground for his play with a polemic on the difference between his type of comedy and that practised by his contemporaries.

In Goldsmith's anonymously published essay *On the Theatre: or, a Comparison between Laughing and Sentimental Comedy* (1773), which acted as a kind of manifesto for *She Stoops*, he expressed strong preferences for the satirical comedy of Ben Jonson and his Restoration heirs over the sentimental comedy that had become very influential in the eighteenth century. While Shakespeare, Jonson and Restoration Comedy all exerted powerful positive influences on Goldsmith's dramatic practice, he was strongly opposed to the negative effects of what has traditionally been described as Sentimentalism on the theatre of his time. The sexual explicitness of Restoration comedy and satirical bite of early-eighteenth-century dramatists, such as John Gay (1685–1732) and Henry Fielding (1707–54), had helped to fuel a negative reaction in favour of a morally uplifting form of drama exhibiting so-called sentimental characteristics. Apart from showing situations and characters that were meant to elicit sympathy rather than ridicule, as in the most famous example *The Conscious Lovers* (1722) by Richard Steele (1672–1729), sentimental drama tended to resolve itself into the characters striking poses while mouthing moral sentiments, but failing to act upon them. In *The School for Scandal* (1777), Richard Brinsley Sheridan (1751–1816) pinpoints the issue with the memorably hypocritical 'man of sentiment', Joseph Surface, whose benevolence turns out to be as superficial as his name suggests. Both Sheridan and Goldsmith were reacting against the excesses of Sentimentalism, but neither of the two powerful London theatre managers at the time, David Garrick (1719–79) or George Colman the Elder (1732–94), was enthusiastic about the idea of staging *She Stoops*. Goldsmith talks in his Dedication of the play to Doctor Johnson about Colman's reluctance and the danger of 'undertaking a comedy, not merely sentimental' (Goldsmith [1773] 1999: 3).

The basic premise of *She Stoops to Conquer* is reminiscent of classical precedent, as well as, apparently, of Goldsmith's own misfortune in once mistaking a gentleman's house for an inn. Hardcastle and Sir Charles Marlow, the two fathers in *She Stoops*, are old friends and want their offspring to marry, just as,

before the action begins, Nikeratos and Demeas, the fathers in
Menander's *Samia*, had intended their offspring to marry. The
obstacles to a marriage of true minds in *She Stoops* stem from
the workings of a society that prescribes a way of proceeding
for male–female relationships that actively prevents them from
succeeding. Ideas of marriages and romantic unions entered into
by two individuals based on mutual love may still predominate
in twenty-first-century Western society, but they are by no means
universal, historically, geographically or socially. Marriages
arranged by fathers in order to maintain or increase their family
fortunes were unexceptional in the period of *She Stoops to
Conquer*. Hardcastle is an enlightened father because he allows
his daughter to make her own choice whether to accept or reject
a potential suitor when she is presented with someone that her
father has already vetted for his suitability in terms of his capacity
to provide a secure economic basis for her and their children.

The mistakes of a night that constitute the plot of the play
stem first from young Marlow, the hero, and his friend Hastings
getting lost in their journey to Hardcastle's house in the
country. Unfortunately, they end up in an ale house, The Three
Pigeons, where Tony Lumpkin, Mrs Hardcastle's son by her
first husband, is engaged in boisterous drinking and, annoyed
by Marlow's unwitting description of him as a drunkard,
misleads the gentlemen from London into thinking that his
stepfather's house is an inn where they can get lodgings for the
night. Once the trap is set, the young gentleman and Hardcastle
find themselves at cross-purposes since each party believes that
they are behaving properly towards the other party but in fact
succeed only in enraging each other by their behaviour. The
mistake about the nature of the location and its class position
as a commercial enterprise rather than a gentleman's house is
compounded by another plot contrivance. Kate, the daughter
Marlow is supposed to woo, is prevented by her father from
dressing fashionably in the evening, just as in *A Bold Stroke
for a Wife* Anne Lovely is forced by her guardian, Obadiah
Prim, to adopt the dress of a Quaker. This means that Marlow
treats Kate quite differently when he mistakes her for a servant

in the supposed inn as opposed to the way that he treats her when she is dressed fashionably and appropriately to her social class. Marlow's different treatment of the two women who are actually the same woman reveals the central inadequacy of the socially sanctioned ways of dealing with women of different classes. Marlow himself is acutely aware of the split in his pattern of behaviour: 'I don't know that I was ever familiarly acquainted with a single modest woman – except my mother – But among females of another class you know.' His friend Hastings points out his problem with modest women: 'If you could but say half the fine things to them that I have heard you lavish upon the barmaid of an inn or even a college bedmaker' (Goldsmith [1773] 1999: 25–6) and the situation is set up for a richly comic scene in which Marlow splutters and misfires vocally throughout an interview with Kate in her finery, unable to even look her in the face.

Marlow is clearly financially eligible to be Kate's husband but, having been educated in single-sex schools and colleges and choosing to spend his leisure time in inns, he is a prime example of the double standard of sexual morality. He has no way of dealing with women except as goddesses or whores. However, throughout the play he is presented as being aware of this and as being unhappy with this aspect of his personality. There is an implicit underlying irony in the presentation of his two courtships of the same woman in different clothes that both marriage (which is seen as only the proper male–female relationship) and implied prostitution (which is seen as improper) are presented as relying heavily on separate economic bargains. Marlow clearly operates by different sets of values, not only when dealing with Kate in her two dresses, but also in his general dealings with those who appear to be of lower social station than himself. Kate, however, consciously adopts roles in order to perform the necessary therapy which will make Marlow into a whole man. Marlow wants to unite the two sides of his personality so he can treat women as people. What one might call the therapeutic power of the female protagonist in acting as the healer who reconciles two apparently contradictory elements as in *As You Like It*, *Twelfth Night* or *She Stoops to Conquer* also rests on a kind of implicit equation that the heroine's attraction to the male beloved is a guarantee of his worthiness, which is tested through her disguised encounters with the object of her affections. At the end of the play, confronted with the inescapable fact that the barmaid and the sober sentimental lady are the same woman, Marlow is forced to realize that it is possible to adopt a different and more wholesome approach in which his two approaches to women need not be in conflict. On a full stage Goldsmith then chooses to banish him and Kate to the back of the stage, 'she tormenting him' (Goldsmith [1773] 1999: 93), to clear the way for other revelations that will facilitate Hastings marrying Constance and Tony Lumpkin not marrying anyone.

She Stoops attacks the fashion for Sentimentalism in several ways. Goldsmith includes characters (particularly Tony) and scenes that a sentimentalist would regard as vulgar, such as the drinking scene in The Three Pigeons inn where lowlife characters behave in an uncouth fashion, although he also satirizes Sentimentalism within that scene, with the mention of the dancing bear that only dances to genteel tunes. When Goldsmith uses scenes and characters that draw on the sentimental tradition, he embeds them in a matrix of contrasting perspectives. He satirizes the sentimental directly in scenes such as Marlow's wooing of Kate in her fine dress, where hypocrisy is foregrounded, and the cult of sentimentality is exposed as a sham. Hastings and Constance are the foils to Kate and Marlow in their own attempts to arrive at a marriage but there is no serious opposition to their pairing from any other romantic interest, except in the eyes of Mrs Hardcastle as she tries to promote Tony as a potential suitor for Constance. Unfortunately for Constance and Hastings, the death of Constance's father has allowed Mrs Hardcastle to assume the role of guardian and defender of the worst kind of patriarchal control in cutting off Hastings's legitimate courtship of Constance, in favour of her own mercenary aspirations for her son, Tony. Although there has been little interest in approaching *She Stoops* in terms of inclusive casting, it is not altogether unsurprising that Constance, an outsider whose own family are out of the picture, has been played at least once by a female mixed-race actor, Cush Jumbo, in 2016 (Figure 4). To judge from the reviews, this colour-blind casting does not seem to have made any kind of impact.

Figure 4 She Stoops to Conquer *by Oliver Goldsmith, directed by Jamie Lloyd. Cush Jumbo (as Constance), Katherine Kelly (as Kate) in the middle of her 'sober-sentimental' encounter with Harry Hadden-Paton (as Charles Marlow); John Heffernan (as Hastings). National Theatre, London, UK; 2011. Credit: Johan Persson/ArenaPAL; www. arenapal.com*

The play's overall impact is heightened by the ways in which the skirmishes between Kate and Marlow are surrounded by groups of characters who are placed at different points on a spectrum to reinforce Goldsmith's development of the plot and to offer systematic structural contrasts and comparisons with their developing relationship, using education, sentiment and the country as touchstones in the process. Constance and Hastings, who are given to behaving in a rather prim fashion and whose languages is quite sententious, are the most straightforwardly sentimental characters in the play, contrasting with Tony (savage and uneducated, given to straight talking and his own pleasure), the stereotyped English country squire. Goldsmith's dramatic method reinforces the play's central preoccupation with the importance and necessity of discovering true natures and true identities. In the middle are Kate and Marlow, two characters who are able ultimately to transcend stereotype by uniting two contradictory sets of characteristics to create whole people as they perform their courtship manoeuvres throughout the play.

This dance does not, of course, take them into a fully developed mature relationship, but it does clear the ground for one, as well as giving them shared experience on which to build. Tony, Marlow and Hastings represent three possible ways in which a young man might behave: Tony is a wild roaring prankster out of parental control and ruined by his lack of education; Hastings is a sentimental and conventional lover; Marlow, ruined by his education in a different way to Tony, oscillates wildly between the two extremes. Moreover, Tony is almost a force of nature who corrects the pretentious behaviour of the town by setting up his pranks and intervenes to help the conventional lovers Hastings and Constance. Like his half-sister Kate, he has a practical way of dealing with issues that contrasts sharply with the more townified manners of Constance, Hastings and Marlow. Similarly, the untutored rustic simplicity of the servants corrects Hardcastle's rhetorical preferences for old things and the ways of the country, while the absurdly metropolitan pretensions of Mrs Hardcastle offer a further angle on the town–country divide as she pretends to a degree of sophistication that makes her an easy target for mockery from the town characters. In *She Stoops* the action raises the suggestion of the corrective power of the country and the whole question of how to arrive at a suitable understanding between two prospective partners via a form of almost-Shakespearian night rule involving the inversion of the rules of both town and daylight. Here there is scarcely any patriarchal objection once the identities of the protagonists are actually revealed to one another when the fathers intervene in the meeting between Kate and young Marlow. This physical unmasking leads onto a deeper psychological unmasking that in turn leads to the necessary rapprochement that permits the action to conclude successfully.

The double wooing plot in *She Stoops* is diffused among the available young people with no-one, except perhaps Mrs Hardcastle, taking Tony seriously as a potential husband for Constance, while his own ambitions extend no further than the offstage Bet Bouncer, so the traditional love triangle of Romantic Comedy is actually made up of four personas in two bodies: the rake Marlow and the barmaid Kate and the demure Marlow and the fine lady Kate. *She Stoops* also uses its farcical and romantic elements to explore the realities underlying the various deceptions using dramatic irony, the pleasure that the audience feels in being more aware of the facts than the characters are, as a way of exploring the discrepancies between reality and appearances. In *She Stoops* the various mistakes about locations lead the characters, particularly Marlow, to adopt behaviour that is clearly inappropriate to its actual context rather than just its supposed one. That new context in turn reveals that such behaviour is inappropriate to any context, because it treats people as stereotypes rather than individuals. Only when the various mistaken identities and locations are revealed can Marlow's split personalities be reconciled, and a new synthesis emerge to replace the old failed system. Because of this interrogative element, good Comedy of Manners like *She Stoops to Conquer* survives even after the actual manners depicted and mocked have long since vanished. The basic questions the play asks remain important: how should people behave towards each other, and how can society's patterns adequately reflect people's real needs and aspirations? The ending of the play is not simply one in which the mistakes of the night are corrected, it is one in which the leading characters have undergone significant change and in which a new and better order has emerged from the old.

The play's ending is itself an attack on the sentimental mode. When Mrs Hardcastle draws attention to the return of the would-be eloping lovers, Constance and Hastings playing pretty straight and earning (not without some justice) Mrs Hardcastle's condemnation of their conduct and Constance's discourse as being like the whining end of a modern novel, she firmly locates the conventional lovers within the sentimental tradition. The discoveries in the last act untie the knots that the plot has ended up in and enable the protagonists to marry whom they want to. The only character who appears to stand outside the comic resolution is Mrs Hardcastle herself, who may have had the stuffing knocked out of her by her cross-country journey and may have become an object of ridicule when she mistakes her husband for a highwayman, but, at the end, she shows no sign of joining in the general rejoicing.

Romantic Comedies often resolve their plot complications by a discovery that the lower-class beloved is in fact a princess in disguise or that a supposed legal prohibition is unenforceable. In the case of *She Stoops* when the supposed barmaid is discovered to be an heiress, the putative barriers to a viable marriage are revealed as spurious in a scene that partly parodies a traditional discovery but also accesses some of its traditional power. In the case of Tony Lumpkin, the confirmation that he is old enough to marry would traditionally allow him to choose a beloved who has previously been beyond his reach as a spouse. Here, using the language of the law and its documents, he is able to formally reject her, thus clearing the way for her to marry her beloved, Hastings.

Many Romantic Comedies involve twists and turns in which four young people oscillate between potential partners but in *She Stoops* there is a remarkable lack of romantic discomfort about any other potential pairings since Hastings and Constance are already established as a couple and there is nowhere and no-one else available to Marlow and Kate, while it is obvious from very early on in the action that Hastings has no reason to be jealous of Tony Lumpkin, his supposed rival for Constance. Goldsmith has created a world in which Tony is incorrigible and, in Sentimental terms, easily the lowest character in the play, but, at the end, Goldsmith's comic universe recognizes that no amount of his mother making him waistcoats could make Tony Lumpkin genteel. A far from noble savage, Tony is liberated from his mother's tyranny and left free to squander his fortune on horses, dogs, drink and Bet Bouncer.

Throughout a staging of the play, the audience is placed in the familiar position of knowing much more about the characters and the action than the characters do themselves. Almost without exception, we are placed in a position of omniscience about the subterfuges and mistakes that characterize the play. From the beginning we know that Old Hardcastle is not an innkeeper, nor is his house an inn, that Kate is neither barmaid nor poor relation, and the bottom of the garden is not Crackskull Common. Only Tony having arrived at the age of maturity is concealed from us, so there is nothing to concern us negatively as the plot unfolds.

Enlightenment and discovery mean that the end of the action what had seemed irreconcilable at the beginning of the play, can be resolved into a comic synthesis in which Marlow and Kate recognize (literally and figuratively) who each other really are and achieve a mutual understanding that will allow them the potential of a happy marriage. The continuing success of the play in the modern world may stem in part from the pleasure audiences get from being able to read the social and theatrical codes more effectively than the characters. Perhaps we also derive pleasure from watching characters discover a 'real' identity that enables them to make sense of their lives because this, in turn, helps us to imagine a wholeness in our own lives. The play's comic exploration of important questions of identity and self-discovery makes a major contribution to its success. Its subtitle, 'the mistakes of a night', could be readily applied to other plays explored in this book and it is indicative of the important fact that drama and night both operate by different rules to those of wakefulness and daylight, in ways that can act as a significant corrective to the burden of the quotidian.

London Assurance

Traditional Romantic Comedy conventions continued to be highly important into the Victorian period. *London Assurance* (1841) demonstrates how a careful exploitation of those tropes and devices could produce a highly successful example of the genre. It was Dion Boucicault's first play, and it was developed throughout rehearsal by Eliza Vestris and Charles Matthews, a very experienced married couple of actor-managers, who were highly skilled at shaping a work to foreground perennially popular themes to elicit maximum comic effect. The continued popular success of works that draw on the features that characterize Romantic Comedy suggests that at some level these plays are accessing powerful archetypes. Boucicault's work, for example, has many parallels with aspects of Roman comedy, the plays of Ben Jonson, English Restoration comedy and the work of Oliver Goldsmith at the end of the eighteenth century. If theoreticians of comedy are right to locate our recurring pleasure at witnessing the various theatrical triumphs of young lovers over all obstacles in a social and psychical need for validation of the ordering of experience and the organization of social existence, then the fact that *London Assurance* draws very directly on a familiar theatrical storehouse of stock elements, plots, motifs and modes of characterization that are familiar from generations of comedies, may explain something of the play's appeal.

London Assurance begins in London with Charles, the dissolute son of Sir Harcourt Courtly, returning very late from a night on the town, accompanied by a new friend Dazzle. Charles's father is to marry Grace, the daughter of his old friend Max, and all the town characters decamp to Gloucestershire for the betrothal where romantic complications ensue. Harcourt is stricken by Gay Spanker and wants to elope with her, Charles pretends to be the completely fictitious Augustus Hamilton and woos Grace, and thus the plots develop. The characters are drawn from an instantly recognizable stock of stereotypes, from would-be wits, foolish old suitors with designs on young heiresses, and the truly witty, to caricature lawyers. Boucicault continued the practice of naming his characters in line with the formulas developed from Ben Jonson's Comedy of Humours (Jonson himself is mentioned in the play) through the Restoration to Goldsmith and beyond, and several of the characters have specific nominal links with characters in other plays. The father and son would-be lovers are surnamed Courtly, which suggests what they are doing in the play, but their first names are Harcourt and Charles. Harcourt recalls Frank Harcourt in *The Country Wife*, whose attempt to woo Alithea is also beset with difficulties, although he wins through in the end. The name Charles recalls another Charles, whose journey to the country results in many of the 'mistakes of the night' in *She Stoops to Conquer*. The name Gay Spanker may need some unpacking for a modern audience since she is jolly rather than gay in the modern sense, and she is rather more of a 'good sport' than she is an SM practitioner. Grace embodies that virtue, Grace's maid, Pert, is pert, the lawyer, Meddle, meddles and Max's surname Harkaway is a hunting call that emphasizes his country-squire approach to life. One curious fact about the negatively stereotypical Jewish creditor Solomon Isaacs is that his complete name is borrowed in Noël Coward's *Private Lives*, where Amanda and Elyot use the name as their safe word to use if they want to stop one of their frequent arguments escalating out of control.

As a comedy that deals with the business of shepherding its young people into an appropriate marriage and defeating an old fool, *London Assurance* can be seen in familiar terms as presenting and investigating the social customs of a leisured class that superficially is concerned with little other than games, fashion and etiquette. However, it uses its exploration of the realities of courtship and marriage as a means of discovering how society can organize itself effectively. Families are usually valued as a prime element in social organization and a social good, so it is inevitable that one of the key elements of comedy will lie in a scrutiny of the fissures between romantic and pragmatic views of marriage. If a family is concerned with

maintaining and enhancing its wealth, then who its sons
and daughters marry becomes a key element in strategies for
preservation of existing capital and safe-guarding its growth.
At this point discrepancies can arise between the family's
financial imperatives and the aspirations of individuals that
need to be reconciled if stable unions, and, by extension, stable
societies are to ensue. In *London Assurance*, the advantages all
initially appear to lie on the side of the parents' generation as
the elderly Harcourt is on the point of engagement to Grace.
Although, he is in fact old enough to be her grandfather, Grace
offers him not only rejuvenation through her youth and beauty
but also the attractions of a more than healthy dowry. In a
frank discussion with her maid, Pert, Grace declares: 'Marriage
matters are conducted nowadays in a most mercantile
manner; consequently a previous acquaintance is by no means
indispensable' (Boucicault [1858] in Griffiths 2010: 26). This
chimes with one of the perennial issues of Romantic Comedy,
the relationship between love and money, that is familiar both
from comments such as Samuel Butler's that marriage was a
manifestation of trade and from plays such as *The Way of the
World*. We may be puzzled by the rejection of the possibility
of romance in Grace's comments and by her apparent
acquiescence in the inherently mercantile status of marriage for
a woman of her age and class. Similarly for a modern reader or
audience, the fact that the engaged couple have never met can
seem highly problematic, but we can already anticipate that
the machinery of comedy will operate to present her with a
more suitable partner than Harcourt and that she will discover
an agency that allows her much more say in determining her
eventual marital fate.

In reading *London Assurance*, we are quite likely to be
aware of some of its problematic features, such as untidy
plotting and characters who disappear after a brief appearance
that had hinted at a subplot, but in performance many of these
issues fade away in the face of the swift moving of the plot,
the exuberance of characterization and the author's delight in
language that means we simply do not have time to raise any

objections about lack of verisimilitude and the like. The most improbable development in the plot is surely when Harcourt is bamboozled into the belief that 'Augustus Hamilton' (another suitor for Grace, who is actually Harcourt's son Charles in disguise) is not in fact his son. However, the play has previously emphasized Harcourt's obtuseness, vanity and foolishness, and the plot leaves no time to dwell on him being deceived because the action moves on swiftly incorporating this mistaken identity premise into the unfolding action.

The play's title, *London Assurance*, opens up the perennial question of the traditional contrast between the values of the town and the values of the country. Particularly in the opening scene, the term 'London Assurance' appears to suggest various quite unsavoury qualities in Charles Courtly that will be challenged in the move to the country. His father, Harcourt, also manifests some of the worst aspects of London assurance in his physical vanity that is captured by his use of a wig and rouge, but also in his determination to pretend to be much more youthful than he is. In Restoration terms Harcourt's chronic narcissism marks him out as a would-be wit who will be punished for his affectation to wit rather than him being a true wit. He is forced into a recognition of his follies less from the collapse of his attempt to elope with Gay and more from the fact he overhears what other characters really think of him. Boucicault, however, treats him more kindly than one might expect. Even after his exposure, Grace is still willing to enlist him in the plot against his own son and he will ultimately be allowed the (faint) possibility that Gay does actually fancy him when her response to his question 'And you still love me?' is 'As much as ever I did' (Boucicault [1858] in Griffiths 2010: 108). Moreover, he is allowed the privilege of giving the closing definition of the nature of a gentleman, which suggests he has managed to transcend his foppery and meretricious pretension to become worthy of delivering the play's conclusion, unless the audience regards him as so obviously unfitted for the role that he undermines that conclusion.

Harcourt is, to some extent, subject to the traditional process in which a London rake is converted to a better person, but, although in his case the visit to the country does change him for the better, there is no strong sense of the country as an environment that challenges town values in favour of a simpler, more apparently honest approach to life. *London Assurance*, however, does stay completely within such a framework, and it is significant that the original title was 'Out of Town', which certainly looks back to the action of *She Stoops* and anticipates that of *The Importance of Being Earnest*. In rehearsal, Vestris suggested the current title, which seems to encapsulate better the many examples of bad behaviour from the townsfolk. The original staging certainly did not encourage audiences to identify with any notion of the therapeutic power of the wild countryside. Innovatively realistic scenery may have helped to persuade an audience of the verisimilitude of actions as well as environment, but there is nothing offered to suggest the traditionally redemptive power of the countryside. We move from the resolutely metropolitan ambience of the Courtly home in Belgrave Square to Oak Hall in Gloucestershire, which suggests the traditional English woodland environment with the dwelling either made of oaks or occupying a space in a traditional English forest. Instead, it is a cultivated area, the lawn of Oak Hall. Moreover this tamed landscape appears for only one act and then gives way to two further domestic settings, a morning room graced with 'handsome pier-glasses, ottomans, etc' and a 'handsome drawing-room', neither of which suggests the country like the Hardcastles' 'old fashioned house' in *She Stoops* (Boucicault, [1840] 2010: 47, 68; Goldsmith. [1773] 1999: 22). Nor are there are any simple rural types to correct metropolitan pretensions: in the first rural scene, Pert, the first person who speaks in the country, is a traditional lady's maid/confidante and the attorney, Meddle, who is always looking for an angle that he can turn to his own profit, offer little to disabuse anyone who conflates town and country into simply the way of the world.

Charles Courtney (and Augustus Hamilton) is very direct descendant of Charles Marlow from *She Stoops to Conquer*, although this Charles deliberately creates his second identity to give him more room to manoeuvre in his amatory escapades with the important proviso that in his case one of his identities is deliberately manufactured rather than real. He is ready to be educated by a woman who takes on the role of a tutor to show him the correct way to behave as a lover in a scene that probably derives some of its effectiveness from its resemblance to such moments as the proviso scene familiar from *The Way of the World*. Like Goldsmith's Kate, Grace is able to tame her lover because she has a better understanding of the ways of the world and sees beneath his disguises and also, pragmatically, because unknown to him she hears the crucial exchange between Gay and Charles at the end of Act Four in which Charles says 'I will bend the haughty Grace', to which her response, unheard by Charles, is the curtain line of the fourth act: 'Will you?' (Boucicault [1858] in Griffiths 2010: 87). The staging here frames her as the true manipulator of plots, who will succeed in taming Charles in Act Five. Unlike many Romantic Comedy endings, her success involves more than reconciling apparently competing plot strands because not only does she get her man, she also pays his debts, a reminder that she is master of his fortunes as well as his emotions as well as a telling reminder that, while the course of true love may not always run smooth, a sensible heroine guards her future and her fortune.

The Importance of Being Earnest

By the end of the century a range of societal and theatrical forces challenged the virtual monopoly power of the tropes and characters that had long characterized English Romantic Comedy. In *The Importance of Being Earnest* (1895) Oscar Wilde exploited those elements to create a work that simultaneously exposed the tenuousness of the values by which society claimed to live and plugged into the genre in ways that allowed his play to scintillate, both as an example of the genre and also as a satire on it. The play deploys many of the familiar tropes of romance in many of its situations. On the face of it, the story involves a familiar working-out of which young woman will marry which eligible young man, a situation complicated by the fact that both the women have determined to marry only someone called Ernest. The plot is complicated both by the fact that neither of the relevant men is (apparently) called Ernest and by the inability of Jack Worthing to provide a convincing explain of who he actually is. The obstacles to appropriate marriages are largely focused on the gorgon-like figure of Lady Bracknell who has engrossed a whole range of patriarchal attitudes that place her squarely in a position to thwart the plans of the young lovers. Jack is a variation on the prince exposed in a hostile environment, in this case, the handbag left at the railway station, whose true identity is only revealed by a miraculous series of coincidences that uncover the truth and facilitate an appropriate marriage, when he turns out to have inadvertently been telling the truth about his name being Ernest. Of course, the ending involves one of the kinds of fudges that characterize the genre: one couple will have to learn to come to terms with the fact that the man is not Ernest, but this simply does not seem to be an issue in production.

The majority of the plays we have examined thus far have heroines who remain largely passive in terms of their ability to influence their fates. However lively or active the heroines may be, they are not, on the face of it, equipped to lead independent lives and their opportunities to live or even to work outside their parental or marital homes are limited by social conventions and assumptions that preclude them from any kind of enterprise or activity outside a very narrow boundary. To a great extent this lack of agency reflects the realities of the external conditions in the societies that are depicted in the plays. In Romantic Comedies, the activities of sexually eligible young women are confined (often literally) to separate spheres of life or are controlled by fathers and father figures who see their roles as ensuring that estates are disposed of to the right kinds of male spouse. In terms of their ability to sustain a lifestyle deemed appropriate for the young woman, such spouses require parental approval, sufficient social status and a suitable fortune. The future happiness of these young women, however, is dependent on some kind of heroic male figure who can breach whatever defences have been constructed by the agents of patriarchy to limit the women's freedom so they can make romantic choices of their own. Of course, some of these women adopt male disguises to transcend the perceived limitations of their roles. Some of them may adopt disguises as working women such as barmaids in a way that obscures their class position in order to achieve a desired end, as in *Twelfth Night* and *She Stoops to Conquer*. But these will only be steps on their way to achieving an appropriate marital status that satisfies both their and their fathers' demands.

3

Romantic Comedies of (Bad) Manners: 1912 to the present

Contexts

The Romantic Comedy tradition continues to exert a powerful influence on theatre, film and television and it reinvents itself from time to time as social expectations change. However, one of the key strands is always the question of who is allowed to form a romantic liaison with whom, who or what tries to thwart this process and how a society finds a way through the dilemmas that stand in the way of true love. In looking at the works of the last century and the present I have chosen to concentrate on those works that broaden the scope of the genre in some way, either by extending the types of characters considered in the main stories or by offering situations that could not previously have been considered within the genre.

By the end of the nineteenth century, with all the changes associated with the Industrial Revolution it had become much easier for young women to achieve a degree of emancipation from the power of the family by undertaking paid roles outside the home. The growth of employment possibilities for women with certain skills included positions for shop assistants, office workers, teachers and factory workers in particular. Similarly, the number of plays in which women outside the gentry were deemed suitable for extended dramatic treatment also grew and the tendency to concentrate solely on the wealthy young gave way to a more complex picture that acknowledged working women as suitable cases for depiction. The changing status of young women was reflected in what have become to be known as 'New Woman Plays', in which writers, often directly or indirectly influenced by the kinds of problem plays associated with Henrik Ibsen or such home-grown authors as Henry Arthur Jones, Arthur Wing Pinero and Oscar Wilde, tackled social problems as they concerned disaffected women drawn from a relatively wide range of social classes. In the theatre, women with a past history that involved a sexual indiscretion might still be required to sacrifice themselves nobly for the sakes of their daughters (as in Bernard Shaw's *Mrs Warren's Profession*, 1893, staged 1902) but it became possible to tackle some anomalies in the position of women, as authors explored the double standard of sexual morality that prescribed quite different responses towards those men and women who had pre-marital sexual intercourse. One of the reasons why women's honour was held to be synonymous with their chastity and specifically their pre-marital virginity is the idea that onward transmission of property to the male's heir depends on the mother not having had sex with anyone other than the putative father. This is not always explicit in the plays we have been considering, but it is close to the surface in ancient New Comedy, in *A Midsummer Night's Dream* and *She Stoops to Conquer*, where Goldsmith memorably satirizes this double standard in the attitudes of Charles Marlow to Kate Hardcastle as a fine lady and as a barmaid. Changing social conditions opened up new areas for exploring the traditional formulas of Romantic Comedy and led to plays such as *Hindle Wakes* (1912) *Hobson's Choice* (1915) and *Private Lives* (1930) that undercut the traditional bases of Romantic Comedy from within frameworks that allowed searching explorations of the impulse towards Romantic Comedy solutions. They raised the possibility that a woman might reject the safety net of traditional marriage at the cost of rejecting her family and its values, they explored the idea that a strong-willed woman might out-manoeuvre her father, and, eventually, the changes to divorce laws, began to offer an increasing number of women and men an escape from the otherwise inescapable obligations of marriage.

Hindle Wakes

Hindle Wakes, by Stanley Houghton (1881–1913), stands out as one of the earliest plays to deal with the whole question of sexual morality from the viewpoint of a working-class woman who claims for herself the same freedom that was routinely assumed to be the perquisite of men, particularly moneyed men. Fanny Hawthorn, a mill worker, has spent the weekend at the end of Wakes Week in a hotel in Llandudno as man and wife with Alan Jeffcote, the son of the mill owner. Knowing that her actions would provoke serious opprobrium and disgrace if they were discovered, she has arranged for her friend Mary Hollins to post a card from Blackpool, where she is supposed to be staying, in order to mislead her parents. The play opens with her parents Chris and Mrs Hawthorn expecting her return, armed with the knowledge that the unfortunate Mary has been killed in a boating accident. The subterfuge has failed, so Fanny finds herself facing a parental ambush in which her deceit is soon unmasked and piece by piece she is forced into admitting her tryst and, ultimately, who the tryst was with. Her father and Alan's father, the mill owner, had started out at work together and are long-standing friends despite the social gap that has now opened between them. Although the play does not mention it directly, by sharing a room and presumably a bed and having sex with Alan, Fanny has compromised her family and herself by losing her virginity before marriage and, potentially, becoming pregnant. To her parents the only proper solution is for her to marry her lover. In this way her honour will be restored and, implicitly, if the marriage takes place quickly enough, the birthdate of any putative offspring of the encounter can be fudged. The situation, however, is complicated by the class difference between Fanny and Alan, not to mention the fact that he is engaged to Beatrice, the daughter of another wealthy mill owner. This dialogue economically charts the family situation:

> **Christopher:** This is what happens to many a lass, but I never thought to have it happen to a lass of mine!
> **Mrs Hawthorn:** Why didn't you get wed if you were so curious? There's plenty would have had you.
> **Fanny:** Chance is a fine thing. Happen I wouldn't have had them!
> **Mrs Hawthorn:** Happen you'll be sorry for it before long. There's not so many will have you now, if this gets about.
> **Christopher:** *He* ought to wed her.
> **Mrs Hawthorn:** Of course he ought to wed her, and shall too, or I'll know the reason why! Come now, who's the chap?
> **Fanny:** Shan't tell you.
>
> (Houghton [1912] 2012: 38)

The parents' assumption that marriage is the only solution to the perceived dilemma of loss of honour and possible pregnancy is one that would have commanded very wide support at the time and Fanny's truculent recalcitrance is not what would be expected from a woman in her situation:

> **Mrs Hawthorn:** Did he promise to wed you?
> **Fanny:** (*In a low voice.*) No.
> **Mrs Hawthorn:** Why not?
> **Fanny:** Never asked him.
> **Mrs Hawthorn:** You little fool! Have you no common sense at all? What did you do it for if you didn't make him promise to wed you?
>
> (Houghton [1912] 2012: 39)

Both parents think that Alan must have seduced Fanny, but, as the play gradually reveals, the truth is not that simple. At this stage, however, although it is late in the evening, her father is sent off to confront Nat, Alan's father. Fanny's parents debate the potential for turning the situation to their and Fanny's advantage, as Mrs Hawthorn remarks that they won't settle for less than Alan marrying Fanny.

The stage setting for the original production neatly encapsulated the social differences between the families by placing the set for the Hawthorn house within the set for the Jeffcote house. When we meet the Jeffcote parents they are debating the merits of their son and his fiancée Beatrice, unaware of the ironic ways in which their world is to be disrupted. Before the embarrassed Hawthorn can bring himself to reveal that the supposed seducer is Alan, Jeffcote declares that he should marry Fanny and even that he will support the culprit financially as he works at his mill. When the truth is revealed Jeffcote promises that he will treat the Hawthorns right. When Alan eventually appears his father castigates him thus: 'Why hadn't thou the sense to pay for thy pleasures, instead of getting mixed up with a straight girl? I've never kept thee short of brass. And if thou must have a straight girl, thou might have kept off one from the mill. Let alone her father's one of my oldest friends' (Houghton [1912] 2012: 59). The question of the ethics of using a prostitute is not taken further in the play. However, faced with his father's determination that he should marry Fanny, rather than attempt to pay her off, Alan can only bleat that 'I don't want to wed Fanny. I want to wed Beatrice' (Houghton [1912] 2012: 60). The two patriarchs are in agreement that the situation demands that Fanny should marry Alan. Fanny's mother unsurprisingly agrees with this remedy. What remains is for the author to broaden the situation out to take in further angles on what is required. Clearly this is not a traditional Romantic Comedy since the hero and heroine have already had sex without being married. The ways in which their society attempts to deal with the situation rest on traditional responses to similar situations

rather than on the individual lovers' own aspirations, which
have not yet been fully revealed. Although the play deals with
a marked change in social possibility and the heroine is a
worker in control of her own destiny because of her power
to earn money, the traditional social values still apply: Alan
is nearly twenty-five, still lives at home, and is not financially
independent of his father, whereas Fanny, who also still lives
at home, is financially independent, although we never know
her actual age.

The patriarchal consensus does not survive Mrs Jeffcote
being told about what Alan has done. Nat Jeffcote says the
engagement is off because Alan has a greater obligation to
another woman, Mrs Jeffcote asks if he has got married and
Nat says that 'he dispensed with the ceremony' and 'spent
last weekend with a girl at Llandudno'. His wife's immediate
(illuminating) response clearly indicates the ways that she has
bought into the patriarchal moral response: 'The creature!'
and '(*Indignantly.*) Why are such women allowed to exist?'
(Houghton [1912] 2012: 65). Faced with her husband's
suggestion that there is no moral difference between Alan's
and Fanny's actions, Mrs Jeffcote adopts a stance that
backs her son against the as yet unidentified Fanny, citing
both her belief in the double standard of sexual morality and
her objections on class grounds. Nat can see no reasons for
differentiating between the behaviour of the man and the
woman in such cases and reminds her that they too started
out as mill workers like Fanny and her family. Mrs Jeffcote
could see some grounds for Fanny's behaviour if she were a
prostitute but not if she is what the play terms a 'straight girl'.
When she learns Fanny's identity, she suspects her of being an
immoral character or of trying to trap Alan into marriage. She
is determined that her son will not marry into a lower social
class, even though (particularly because?) she too came from
that class. She argues that marriages of this kind are doomed
to fail, but Nat is adamant that marriage is the only possible
solution. When the third patriarch, Tim Farrar, father of Alan's
fiancée Beatrice, appears he at first assumes that the issue is that

someone has spotted him on an illicit excursion to Brighton, but claims there is no moral issue because he is a widower and therefore under no obligations to anyone. Protective of his daughter, he thinks Alan should be punished but values preserving her reputation above the idea of Alan marrying Fanny. A self-made man and, according to the author, 'much the coarsest and commonest person in the play' (Houghton [1912] 2012: 71), he thinks that Fanny and her parents might be suitably bought off but is genuinely puzzled that Nat will only accept Alan marrying Fanny. Quizzed by Tim, Alan states that he does not think it's necessary to marry Fanny and Tim concurs, only to rethink his attitude when Nat threatens to disinherit Alan. His attitudes are both cynical and mercenary as he now decides that Alan has not treated Beatrice right: 'When a chap's engaged he ought to behave himself. From the way thou's been carrying on, thou might be married already' (Houghton [1912] 2012: 79). The irony of the statement is self-evident: Tim is now willing to reject Alan because he will have nothing to offer in the way of a dowry, but Alan believes that Beatrice will still accept him for himself, thus paving the way for a long-anticipated first appearance for Beatrice and their inevitable confrontation. By now we have been offered a series of parental attitudes towards the escapade and also Alan's defence of his actions, but we have not yet heard at all from Beatrice and only a little from Fanny.

Unsurprisingly, Alan flounders as he attempts to find a justification for his double standards, while Beatrice, brought up conventionally pious, wonders which of Alan's base and horrible feelings for Fanny and his 'higher – finer' feelings for her are 'most like love' (Houghton [1912] 2012: 84). She admits that, despite everything, she still loves him and succumbs to his advances when 'he seizes her violently and kisses her several times. She yields to him and returns his embrace' (Houghton [1912] 2012: 88). However, Beatrice is adamant that Fanny has the better claim on him because of their dalliance and declares that she will not marry him. The parents of the illicit lovers then begin planning the wedding with no input from

the couple at all until Alan wonders what Fanny has to say
about the arrangements, and she states that '[i]t doesn't suit
me to let you settle my affairs without so much as consulting
me' (Houghton [1912] 2012: 97) and that she has no intention
of marrying Alan. Left to themselves, Fanny reveals the truth
about their affair to Alan. She regards him as suitable for a
liaison but not as a marriage partner: 'You're a man, and I was
your little fancy. Well I'm a woman, and *you* were *my* little
fancy' (Houghton [1912] 2012: 104). Alan finds this immoral
and is dismayed at Fanny's final judgement of him: 'You're not
a fool altogether. But there's summat lacking. You're not man
enough for me. You're a nice lad, and I'm fond of you. But I
couldn't ever marry you' (Houghton [1912] 2012: 105). When
Fanny's mother is told that she will not marry Alan, she shows
how far she has assimilated patriarchal attitudes, condemning
her for choosing 'to be a girl who's lost her reputation, instead
of letting Alan make you into an honest woman' (Houghton
[1912] 2012: 106), but Fanny fails to see how marrying the
man her mother called a blackguard earlier would make her
into an honest woman. Determined to exercise her power,
Mrs Hawthorn will no longer countenance Fanny staying in
the family home, but Fanny claims her independence anyway:
'[S]o long as there's weaving sheds in Lancashire I shall earn
enough brass to keep me going. I wouldn't live at home again
after this, not anyhow' (Houghton [1912] 2012: 107). The play
ends with Alan going off to ask Beatrice to marry him, Jeffcote
musing that '[w]omen are queer folk! Who'd have thought that
Fanny would refuse to wed him?' (Houghton [1912] 2012:
108) and Mrs Jeffcote finding something providential in the
way things have turned out.

Hindle Wakes lays bare the skeleton of social and moral
beliefs that underlie whole swathes of the Romantic Comedy
tradition, with its exposure of the double standard of
sexual morality as it applies to what men may do and what
women may do. It skewers patriarchal values and shows
how the class system is upheld by both men and women
who have internalized those values. The play recognizes the

many subterfuges and hypocrisies that underpin not just the parochial morality of a particular period and a specific locality, but also long-lasting traditions sanctified by many societies and in many countries. It was scandalous at the time of its first production for its openness about sexual matters with its overt references to prostitution and its scarcely veiled suggestions that Fanny might have got pregnant in her weekend away. It is not a traditional Romantic Comedy since the heroine and her lover are not destined to become man and wife. Indeed, their 'failure' to marry is a happy end as is Fanny's Ibsen-like declaration of her own independence. Moreover, not only is any forthcoming marriage postponed well beyond the end of the play, but it is also dependent on Beatrice deciding that Alan is worth having as a husband, in the face of what many audiences might regard as his abundant faults and few virtues. Nevertheless, the play depends for much of its power on a recognition that its underlying skeleton is based on the Romantic Comedy tradition as the way in which a society finds ways of channelling the disruptive power of love and sex into acceptable social arrangements.

The play started many debates among its original audiences because it touched on so many issues in contemporary society. It was welcomed by many as a remarkable dissection of the double standard of sexual morality that castigated women who dared to behave as men did and was rightly applauded for its openness. The broadly socialist newspaper *The Clarion* is not untypical of those that favoured the play:

> The great moment of the play comes when Fanny – the sinning or sinned against Fanny – refuses to be made an honest woman by marrying a man she neither loves nor respects. She refuses not only to be converted into an honest woman, but also to convert Alan into an honest and moral young man – at her expense. She had but looked upon him as a pastime, the sort of chap one could have a bit of fun with and not bother about again. Word for word, she repeats often what he has previously said about her.

> Naturally he is very much shocked, because, as he says,
> she is a woman, and may not do these things – not for the fun
> of it, but allowable only if she loves the man! Ye gods! Where
> *is* the distinction? Yet it is a distinction admitted by so many.
>   (*Clarion*: 4 October 1912)

The *Pall Mall Gazette* also recognized the significance of the play: '[T]he character of Fanny in her strength and independence is new to the stage, and is immensely refreshing' (17 July). The newspaper then became host to a lengthy sustained controversy in which the author and the actor playing Fanny (Edyth Goodall) were involved. Several correspondents found the play disgusting, others objected to its perceived immorality and some accused it of being too reticent in how it discussed the potential practical consequences of such an encounter. One correspondent objected that 'no one seems to have the slightest fear of any material results from this weekend at Llandudno' (6 August), another thought that 'the cool way in which possible maternity is kept out of sight' was enough 'to render the play worthless' (7 August), although the play does in fact make carefully worded references to the possibility of pregnancy and to the fact that other similar situations had led to pregnancy, while the whole premise that the couple should marry is aimed at restoring what would conventionally be regarded as honour to a dishonourable situation. When Houghton responded to the correspondence, he pointed out that '[t]he point is a difficult one to deal with in a play, and it is hardly less difficult here; but I may remind your innocent correspondent that possible maternity is frequently kept out of sight in a very cool way indeed' (12 August). What is very surprising is the sheer amount of argument in responses to the play about its verisimilitude or otherwise, with correspondence sometimes even accusing Houghton of having deliberately falsified Fanny's back story. Others questioned whether an actress could possibly play the part of Fanny without being corrupted by it, eliciting a brisk demolishing of the negative case from Goodall. The play certainly pushes the boundaries of what was then socially or morally acceptable, a fact that was recognized in responses to the productions that occurred in the late twentieth century and around the play's centenary.

Hobson's Choice

Figure 5 Hobson's Choice *by Harold Brighouse, directed by Jonathan Church. Naomi Frederick (as Maggie Hobson), Bryan Dick (as Willy Mossop). Vaudeville Theatre, London, UK; 14 June 2016. Credit: Nigel Norrington/ArenaPAL; www.arenapal.com*

Another play from the so-called Lancashire school, *Hobson's Choice* (1915), by Harold Brighouse, operates at the intersection of several traditions. Hobson's Choice is a popular phrase used to describe a situation in which someone is effectively only offered one choice out of a situation. It derives from the practice of one Thomas Hobson, a seventeenth-century Cambridge entrepreneur, whose livery stable only allowed customers to take the first horse offered, in order to ensure a fair allocation of the horses' workload. The play has distinct overtones of a comedic version of *King Lear* as the patriarch Hobson attempts to control his daughters and also of *The Taming of the Shrew* with Maggie Hobson's whirlwind dragooning of Will Glossop into marriage and a successful career as a shoemaker and seller in the face of opposition from her father, who is Will's boss at the beginning of the play. It also inverts the Cinderella story by showing Will being socially elevated because of his skills as a bootmaker. Revived several times around the time of its centenary it also attracted attention from Tanika Gupta in 2003 (revised 2019) who reset it amongst the East African Asian community in Salford in the 1980s, swopping boot-making for sari-making. In the original version, Brighouse makes the benefactor who funds Will's new enterprise a lady who appears in Act One to praise his skills, but in Gupta's version, not only is she the benefactor she is also the doctor who reappears to diagnose old Mr Hobsons's alcoholic dependence and declares that he will need to be looked after by one of his daughters. This change reinforces the sense of Hobson being surrounded by matriarchal figures and allows the young lovers to be blessed by a fairy godmother, perhaps a sentimentalization of the original, perhaps a foregrounding of its debt to fairy-tale conventions.

Several of the plays we are examining here choose to set the action some thirty years before the date of the play, notably both versions of *Hobson's Choice*, *Hindle Wakes* and *East Is East*, while *Rafta Rafta* adapts a play from some forty years previously. Perhaps the point in all these cases is that roughly one generation is supposed to have passed after the action of the play, so that the contemporary audience can be engaged with the roots of their own experience.

In Romantic Comedies from the late nineteenth century onwards the disruption caused by the outsider who cannot be accommodated becomes even more important as the plays explore new obstacles to creating an easy comic synthesis. In *Hindle Wakes* the traditional offer of a resolution that will shore up patriarchy by drafting an unwilling man and woman into a socially acceptable union in marriage is defeated by her (and, to a lesser extent, his) unwillingness to play the game according to the usual rules. Moreover, the traditional emphasis on the union of protagonists who turn out to be from leisured social classes gives way here, and in *Hobson's Choice*, to young people from manufacturing and commercial backgrounds who are making their own way in life. So class itself becomes a much more central issue as the previously marginal moves towards the centre. Similarly other aspects of social order start to make their way into the frame as social change raises significant issues around the questions of race and sexuality.

Private Lives

In the first half of the twentieth century the major extra-theatrical change that allowed innovation in the form of Romantic Comedy was the increased opportunity for divorce, which allowed for the still-limited and often-fraught possibility of ending an unsatisfactory marriage. The 1923 Matrimonial Causes Act, building on the similarly titled 1857 Act, enshrined the possibility of both men and women being able to sue for divorce on the grounds of the other partner's adultery. Divorce had become, if not respectable, much easier to obtain and society was beginning to formulate new approaches to the complex changes associated with new more liberal attitudes to the breakdown of marriage. That these changes coincided with some women in the United Kingdom being given the vote in 1918 and all women aged over twenty-one being allowed to vote from 1928, reflects on the complex social cross-currents that characterized the period after the First World War. *Private Lives* is an interesting example of how to use the framework of Comedy of Manners to explore what a Romantic Comedy could be in the changed social circumstances of the 1920s.

Stanley Cavell has explored the phenomenon of cinematic
marriages that have ended, in his important study of what he
called the 'comedy of remarriage'. He identified this genre in a
range of screwball comedies from the late 1930s to the 1950s.
In these Hollywood comedies, the traditional presentation
of a Romantic Comedy ending with its shorthand of a final
wedding as a token that the couple 'lived happily ever after' is
not available, because the couple have already been married
and are now divorced. According to Cavell, in formal terms,
'The genre of remarriage is an inheritor of the preoccupations
and discoveries of Shakespearean romantic comedy, especially
as that work has been studied by, first among others, Northrop
Frye.' However, unlike traditional Romantic Comedy, 'the
drive of its plot is not to get the central pair together but to get
them *back* together, together *again*. Hence the fact of marriage
in it is subjected to the fact or the threat of divorce.' This
clearly reflects the social realities of both British and American
societies in which the greater availability and more widespread
acceptance of divorce in the early twentieth century makes the
topic more viable in theatrical terms. Much of what Cavell
deals with is already true of other theatrical manifestations of
Romantic Comedy: '[T]he achievement of human happiness
requires not the perennial and full satisfaction of our needs as
they stand but the examination and transformation of these
needs' (4–5). He also claims that 'it will be a virtue of our
heroes to be willing to suffer a certain indignity, as if what
stands in the way of change, psychologically speaking, is a false
dignity; or, socially speaking, as if the dignity of one part of
society is the cause of the opposite part's indignity, a sure sign
of a disordered state of affairs' (Cavell 1981: 1, 1–2, 4–5, 8), a
perception that can be usefully applied across the whole genre.

In fact, despite the apparent similarities of the play to some
of the Hollywood comedies, Cavell's argument specifically
excludes *Private Lives*, which he describes as:

A work patently depicting the divorce and remarrying of a
rich and sophisticated pair who speak intelligently and who

infuriate and appreciate one another more than anyone else. But their witty, sentimental, violent exchanges get nowhere; their makings up never add up to forgiving one another (no place they arrive at is home to them) and they have come from nowhere (their constant reminiscences never add up to a past they can admit together). They are forever stuck in orbit around the foci of desire and contempt. This is a fairly familiar perception of what marriage is. The conversation of what the genre of remarriage is, judging from the films I take to define it, of a sort that leads to acknowledgement; to the reconciliation of a genuine forgiveness; a reconciliation so profound as to require the metamorphosis of death and revival, the achievement of a new perspective on existence; a perspective that presents itself as a place, one removed from the city of confusion and divorce. One model to draw from the structure of *Private Lives* is that no one feature of the genre is sufficient for membership in the genre, not even the title feature of remarriage itself.

(Cavell 1981: 18–19)

I hope to show that Cavell is wrong in his analysis of *Private Lives*, although his exploration of the film genre is both thought-provoking and exemplary. He points the way towards the development of new theatrical manifestations of Romantic Comedy in which the old certainties of patriarchal power in marriage are threatened by changing social and economic realities. *Private Lives* is an example of a dramatist taking the apparently superficial, trivial and empty lifestyle of characters from a moneyed and leisured class and using them to explore the actual ways of the world. Not only do the divorced protagonists, Amanda and Elyot, undergo a journey and a quest for a new synthesis, so too do their new spouses, Victor and Sybil. There is a genuine sense of the absurdity of the characters' lives and of their need to achieve some kind of self-definition that extends its force far beyond the superficial presentation of wittily amoral socialite behaviour. The play shows how the basic concerns of Romantic Comedy remain the important issues of how people can come to terms with their need to relate to each other.

Almost everything the main characters do in *Private Lives* is a violation of accepted social conventions, particularly those that centre on the sacredness and uniqueness of the marriage bond. The play begins soon after the establishment of two marriages, as a result of the dissolution of one, and it ends up with the re-establishment of that first marriage at the expense of the other two. Once again, the comedic pattern of rotation of partners is like a dance that establishes patterns that appear to offer some hope for marital success beyond the end of the play.

The major difference between the social world of this play and that of the others we have examined so far in this book is that the idea of marriage as a single event uniting a couple into a new unity has given way to a new social order in which the possibility of the wedding not being a happy ending is acknowledged by the society depicted in the work. At the time of *Private Lives*, the law allowed couples to divorce for several reasons, including adultery, but there always had to be someone who was deemed to be the guilty party responsible for the breakdown of the marriage. Guilty parties were often men because divorce was potentially much more serious for a woman. This stemmed from the pervasive and long-standing belief that a woman's honour resided solely in her sexual chastity, which meant that a divorcee might lose social status and her place in society, whereas a man's honour was not seen as intrinsically or solely located in his sexual behaviour. This double standard meant that there was soon an established set of cultural practices for couples seeking a divorce to follow. The male partner would provide evidence that he had committed adultery, whether he had or not, by being discovered in a fabricated hotel tryst in bed with a woman who was not his wife, thus providing the necessary 'evidence' of adultery for the courts in order that the couple would be able to get a divorce This explains why Elyot was in the hotel room in Brighton with Vera Williams and her hairbrush.

Marriage is, of course, a great social regulator that marks a transition from one social state to another (single to married), it is associated with the harnessing of sexual drives to social goods, and it is a very highly charged social marker of the creation of a new family unit with all its associated trappings and commitments. This is clearly why Byron thought that all comedies are ended with a marriage and why we are seldom encouraged in Romantic Comedy to explore too closely what exactly hasn't been wrapped up at the end of the play. Does it matter that one of the male lovers in the *Dream* is still enchanted when they wake up in the wood or that Kate and Young Marlow are not heard by the audience for the last minutes of *She Stoops*? How many Ernests are logically required at the end *of The Importance of Being Earnest*? Conversely, would it be easier to read *Measure for Measure* as a Romantic Comedy if Isabella had been given a line to respond positively to the Duke's marriage proposal?

For most of the period covered by the plays selected for this study, English laws of marriage were heavily indebted to Christian theology and today many marriages still take place according to Christian rites. The exact form of these rites has changed over history but for most of the period under consideration, a marriage ceremony conducted in accordance with the rites of the Church of England, the established church in England, included these words:

[Matrimony] is an honourable estate, instituted of God in the time of man's innocency, signifying unto us the mystical union that is betwixt Christ and his Church; … and therefore is not by any to be enterprised, nor taken in hand, unadvisedly, lightly, or wantonly, to satisfy men's carnal lusts and appetites, like brute beasts that have no understanding; but reverently, discreetly, advisedly, soberly, and in the fear of God; duly considering the causes for which Matrimony was ordained. First, It was ordained for the procreation of children …Secondly, It was ordained for a remedy against sin, and to avoid fornication …

> Thirdly, It was ordained for the mutual society, help, and comfort, that the one ought to have of the other, both in prosperity and adversity.
>
> (*Book of Common Prayer*: 1662)

In the marriage ceremony the couple swear to love, honour and comfort one another, for richer or poorer, in sickness or in health. The working assumption is that the outward form, the ceremony, stands as a token of inner truth, which is why one of the most powerful tropes in film Romantic Comedy is the moment when some outside force breaks the ceremony such as in *The Graduate* (1967) or *Four Weddings and a Funeral* (1994). Romantic Comedy of Manners tends to operate in the gaps that reveal the discrepancies between what the wedding ceremony stands for and the actual reality of everyday life. In theory there should be no gap – a mystical union – but in fact it may not work out like that. The comedy of remarriage makes it clear that there may well also be other important issues at stake.

One of the assumptions about marriage is that it will be fertile, and the plays often expend considerable effort on addressing that issue and trying to ensure fertility in the forthcoming marriage, from the wedding blessing in the *Dream* to the discussion of strait lacing in *Way of the World* through to the intimate discussions of ovulation and its potential significance in *Beginning* (2017). However, for much of its history, comedy has chosen not to incorporate children onstage. Of course, ancient Greek and Roman plots can take off from the dilemma that a young woman has given birth, as a result of what we would now call rape, and comic complications ensue until the rapist is revealed to be the eligible young man who already wants to marry her or is actually already married to her, so, although babies can figure in Romantic Comedy, generally children are conspicuous by their absence. There are often elements of play, playfulness and games playing in these works that underpin the sense of a society that is rule-bound in ways that are similar to the ways in which sports are regulated by their own rules that shape what may be done and what may not be done, often, like tennis, practised by precisely the leisured classes who also play the social games called manners or etiquette.

In *Private Lives* the games analogies are underpinned by the formal aspects of the visual elements, particularly the arrangement of Act One set, which is organized in such a way that it resembles a tennis court on which the two couples will play out a game of mixed doubles. The stage is divided down the middle by the physical boundary between the two hotel rooms that serves as a net to divide the two parts of the court from one another, and over which Amanda and Elyot will lob desperate conversational sallies. Coward's exposition is carefully structured to use a whole range of social rituals and conventions to enhance our understanding of the tensions between the individuals and within the couples.

In *Private Lives* these conventions are presented to us within the context of a great social ritual: the first night of the honeymoon, when, after the wedding ceremony itself, the individuals are faced with the complex processes of further refining and fleshing out the accord that brought them together in the first place. The greater social observance provides the frame within which other rituals – cocktails, dressing for dinner and so on – are negotiated. But there is a massive difference from previous Romantic Comedies here, since for two of the four protagonists this is a *second* honeymoon. So, for his early audiences, the situation Coward sets up in these opening skirmishes in *Private Lives* occupies a dangerously transgressive area of untested new societal expectations. Instead of the relaxation of tension that we associate with the expected discovery that there are four eminently eligible potential marriage partners, these four individuals have already arranged themselves into what seem to be socially acceptable pairings. This variation on a standard pattern opens up many avenues for Coward to explore. The ways in which he develops his scenario in the first act indicate that this situation is extremely fragile, but any potential resolution to the dilemma appears likely to be equally transgressive of social norms. *Private Lives* relies on a very small cast (the two couples and a maid) and Coward uses formal patterning within and across the two relationships to create the impression of a complete social code turned inwards on itself. From Menander onwards, the majority of Romantic Comedies where debate, romance, intrigue and mistaken identity form a significant part of the action require a much larger cast. In *She Stoops to Conquer*, for example, there are twenty speaking roles with individual names or functions. So Coward has chosen to create his world by means other than the proliferation of characters, particularly through invoking aspects of the social code in dialogue.

In the opening exchanges we have references to yachts, the custom of dressing for dinner, dancing and playing the piano, all of which conjure up a world of a social elite living a leisured life. The most significant aspect of this exploratory dialogue occurs when Elyot and Sibyl discuss sunbathing and tanning (not yet linguistically differentiated from sunburn):

> **Elyot:** We'll bathe to-morrow morning.
> **Sibyl:** I mustn't get sunburnt.
> **Elyot:** Why not?
> **Sibyl:** I hate it on women
> **Elyot:** Very well, you shan't then. I hope you don't hate it on men.
> **Sibyl:** Of course I don't. It's suitable to men.
>
> (Coward 1934: 471)

Gender roles are clearly located here in terms of the characters' social expectations, even as far as Elyot's '[i]f you feel you'd like me to smoke a pipe, I'll try and master it' (Coward 1934: 471), a curiously bathetic reduction of the traditional idea of the hero undergoing an ordeal to win his beloved to an imagined catastrophe of humiliation and spent matches.

A significant part of the dialogue here centres on the question of divorce and, therefore, the difference between the ritual and societal values of the wedding ceremony, the realities of married life, and the negative rituals of the actual divorce. Elyot's account is acutely aware of the differences between practice and theory: 'She divorced me for cruelty, and flagrant infidelity. I spent a whole week-end at Brighton with a lady called Vera Williams. She had the nastiest looking hairbrush I have ever seen' (Coward 1934: 473). Sybil describes this as '[m]isplaced chivalry', but Elyot indicates that he couldn't divorce Amanda because '[i]t would not have been the action of a gentleman, whatever that may mean' (Coward 1934: 471). So we are given a very strong sense of the existence of certain codes that the characters adhere to, but also a sense that those codes are understood as practices observed rather than practices believed in by both parties. Elyot doesn't know what the action of a gentleman might be and there appears to be a certain unhappiness in him at Sybil's conventional attitude to sunbathing.

When Victor appears it is a brilliantly economical comic device to have him calling out Amanda's name in the form of the shortened endearment 'Mandy', a name that Amanda shows absolutely no sign of accepting. Their initial dialogue continues to suggest this lack of true contact as he compares her to an advertisement, and she complains about the cloth of his suit ('[a] bit hearty isn't it?' [Coward 1934: 475]). The key to the future developments of the tangled situation comes in the paralleled conversations as each couple talks about Elyot and Amanda's previous honeymoon in terms that make the absent partner the guilty one: each considers the nature of their previous and current relationships and both couples talk about sunbathing. Elyot may have been somewhat disappointed with Sybil's conventional attitude to sunbathing, but now Victor and Amanda develop the argument:

Amanda: I want to get a nice sunburn.
Victor (*reproachfully*)**:** Mandy!
Amanda: Why, what's the matter?
Victor: I hate sunburnt women.

Amanda: Why?
Victor: It's somehow, well, unsuitable.

(Coward 1934: 476)

Sybil has already used the word 'suitable' when she says it's suitable for men to be tanned. This demonstrates one of the ways in which the two minor spouses are bought together by their shared vocabulary and their shared attitudes. Sibyl calls Elyot 'Ellie' just as Victor calls Amanda 'Mandy' but neither partner shows any sign of accepting the name. Coward provides signposts in the characters' proper names that point us towards aspects of their characterization in ways that are completely familiar from past practice. Victor appears to be a piece of ironic naming since the character appears to be a loser, according to Coward, although I will argue that he does achieve a kind of victory in the end. Sibyl too relates to her name in terms of her attempts to prophesy (the Sibyls were ancient Roman women priests who voiced oracles) while Amanda derives from the Latin word *amanda*, which means 'deserving to be loved'. Moreover, the point about the suitability of suntans echoes as far back as Menander where Sosastros in the *Dyskolos*, attempts to earn respect from his potential wife's father by labouring in the fields and his reward is simply getting sunburnt. If you are well off and leisured, you can stay out of the sun and preserve your skin from its weathering effects. Thus the growing fashionability of suntans for women in the twentieth century in particular indicates a significant change in social practices, since the tan comes to indicate the availability of leisure time to work on a tan rather than a tan being the necessary negative result of having to work in the open.

Coward organizes these opening dialogues very subtly in order to establish what will turn out to be recurring motifs that provide much of the play's dynamic impetus. We have already seen that the two opening scenes run in carefully structured patterns that complement one another and from the moment Victor calls 'Mandy' we know that a catastrophic social event is inevitable since the couples must collide. The tensions inside each couple foreshadow the inevitable disaster since both couples quarrel about the previous marriage of Elyot and Amanda. Moreover, we find that there are two quite different views of the nature of experience contained within the couples. Both Elyot and Amanda are unconventional: Amanda confesses that she is 'apt to see things the wrong way round', things like '[m]orals. What one should do and what one shouldn't' (Coward 1934: 481) and she doesn't accept being normal is something to be glad about. Victor's worldview, on the contrary, is bounded by normality and by a very static model of experience: 'I couldn't love you more than I do now' he says to which Amanda's reply is 'I did so hope our honeymoon was going to be progressive' (Coward 1934: 476). Chance and change are anathema to Victor whose predilections are essentially conservative and aimed towards stasis. Elyot, on the other hand, is attempting to adapt the values that Victor lives by but without too much success: 'Love is no use unless it's wise, and kind, and undramatic. Something steady and sweet, to smooth out your nerves when you're tired. Something tremendously cosy; and unflurried by scenes and jealousies. That's what I want, what I've always wanted really. Oh my dear, I do hope it's not going to be dull for you' (Coward 1934: 471). The bathetic end of Elyot's speech indicates the effect that the images of order and quiet have already begun to have on his state of mind. Of course, his immediate reaction when he sees Amanda, is, like hers, to flee.

Coward counterpoints what the dialogue says against the characters' feelings, using the constraints of the social code to create tensions when convention prescribes behaviour that runs counter to desire. He also allows the theatrical situation itself to articulate his drama. Thus, the catastrophic meeting between Elliot and Amanda begins wordlessly: we already have the information we need to establish the likely nature of their encounter, so Coward can arrange to show us the two characters reacting physically to a reminder of shared experience as they listen to the familiar song and sing it. Although their dialogue is brief, the length of the musical interlude establishes them firmly as a linked couple, even if the link will not be altogether harmonious. Both Elyot and Amanda propose flight as a remedy for their socially unacceptable predicament and neither is willing to explain to their respective partner why they want to flee. So we find them being linked in their attitudes to the situation, just as Sibyl and Victor are brought together in their determination to stick to prearranged plans. Inevitably the two ideas of how to proceed clash and bring Elyot and Amanda closer together as they contemplate the possibility of a chance encounter on their separate journeys to Paris. As their dialogue continues Coward stresses the importance of human contact without which the whole business of going on a world tour is arid and meaningless. At the end of the act Victor and Sibyl have also begun to move away from their entrenched rigidity as Sibyl, after initially rejecting the social intimacy implied by Victor's first offer of a cocktail, accepts his second offer, while their dialogue about the yacht shows them coming together through their shared small talk.

The difficulty about all the socially prescribed rituals is that they conflict with the characters' aspirations and needs, so the decision by Amanda and Elyot to depart is not just a piece of selfishness (which it is) but also an act of courage in which they recognize their own real needs. At this stage in Act One, however, their understanding is still limited, and they attempt to set boundaries to their behaviour with the invention of the catchphrase 'Solomon Isaacs' which is to be invoked to suspend any quarrels. This name presumably derives from the character in Boucicault's *London Assurance* but its specific significance is obscure.

In some ways the second act is an interlude in terms of Comedy of Manners but not Romantic Comedy, as it shows Elyot and Amanda negotiating several important facets of how they will conduct their interpersonal (romantic) relationships. Perhaps most forcefully, it shows how difficult it can be to deal with individual feelings within prescribed rules. Elyot and Amanda's attempt to regulate their own behaviour by excluding potential sources of disagreement through the verbal formula 'Solomon Isaacs', soon has to be shortened to 'Sollocks' in order to help them police their own relationship. At this stage neither has worked out a suitable way of relating to the other and their new-found relationship seems likely to founder on the usual rock of the double standard for sexual behaviour. Elyot believes that '[i]t doesn't suit women to be promiscuous', but Amanda knows that the truth is '[i]t doesn't suit men for women to be promiscuous' (Coward 1934: 509). As their relationship is explored, it appears that more and more areas of life are going to have to be excluded if Elyot and Amanda are to co-exist. The argument is conducted through aspects of the social code such as drinking, behaviour towards neighbours and so on. It culminates in the very antithesis of polite behaviour – a knockabout fight of considerable venom between the two of them which obliterates all the notions of good behaviour discussed in the first act and provides a splendid act curtain as Victor and Sibyl arrive and stare dumfounded at the spectacle.

It is easy to regard *Private Lives* as a kind of romp that celebrates the worst kind of self-indulgence, but this stems in part from a too ready acceptance of Coward's own statements about Victor and Sibyl. He saw the play as 'a reasonably well-constructed duologue for two experienced performers, with a couple of extra puppets thrown in to assist the plot and to provide contrast.' According to Coward, this left 'a lot to be desired' because of his 'dastardly and conscienceless behaviour towards Sibyl and Victor, the secondary characters. These, poor things, are little better than ninepins, lightly wooden, and only there at all in order to be repeatedly knocked down and stood up again' (Coward 1934: xiii). In fact he took pains to cast the part of Victor very well, hiring the young Laurence Olivier because he felt that the part was weak, and that Olivier could bolster its impact through the force of his acting. However, to see it solely in these terms ignores the true dynamics of the play: all the characters start the play knowing very little about themselves or each other, but the intensity of the relationship that develops between Amanda and Elyot in Act Two indicates a considerable degree of growing awareness. In the more lyrical moments of that act we are presented with the nub of the problem of how to behave in an absurd world. As Elyot says, 'You mustn't be serious, my dear one, it's just what they want. … All the futile moralists who try to make life unbearable. Laugh at them. Be flippant. Laugh at everything, all their sacred shibboleths. Flippancy brings out the acid in their damn sweetness and light' (Coward 1934: 520). The problem we are left with at the end of the act is that this also apparently fails to work: Elyot and Amanda are unable to operate apart and unable to operate together, proposing a dynamic view of life rather than static one, but are unable to keep control of their dynamism, which can be interrupted briefly by the magic words, but which ends up in the uncontrolled struggle at the end of the act.

By the beginning of Act Three, the wronged spouses have exerted their territorial claims by barricading the doors of Elyot's and Amanda's rooms. The majority of the act centres on all the characters having difficulty in finding a way to express their feelings since the social code provides no obvious answers as they attempt to co-exist in the flat. Elyot responds to Victor's complaint about his flippancy with '[h]as it ever struck you that flippancy might cover a very real embarrassment?' which Victor thinks is bad taste. Elyot clinches his argument thus: 'No worse than bluster and invective. As a matter of fact, as far as I know, this situation is entirely without precedent. We have no prescribed etiquette to fall back upon. I shall continue to be flippant' (Coward 1934: 534). The papering-over the cracks that precede the actual breakfast is also concerned with fixing up something like an agreed socially acceptable solution, even in the desperate attempt by Victor to fight Elyot, basically because it would ease his mind. Amanda plays the role of the penitent in her long speech beginning 'I don't expect you to understand', which ends with 'perhaps one day, when all this is dead and done with, you and I might meet and be friends. That's something to hope for, anyhow. Good-bye, Victor dear.'

Figure 6 Private Lives *by Noël Coward, directed by Michael Cabot. Olivia Beardsley (as Sibyl Chase), Jack Hardwick (as Elyot Chase), Helen Keeley (as Amanda Prynne), Kieran Buckeridge (as Victor Prynne). London Classic Theatre at the Theatre Royal Bury St Edmunds, Suffolk, UK; September 2017. Credit: Sheila Burnett/ ArenaPAL; www.arenapal.com*

This speech sounds like something out of a poor melodrama, and it is noteworthy that her very next speech after the briefest of comments from Victor is in a completely different register: 'I'd rather marry a boa constrictor' (Coward 1934: 545).

When the two couples eat breakfast, the food and the passing of drinks provide weapons for their debates (Figure 6). Amanda's desperate small talk is counterbalanced by Elyot's determination to subvert it, finally regaining Amanda's attention by his capping of her foreign travel story. He breaks up the story by referring to impolite behaviour – making strange noises after eating strange food – and thus causing Amanda to choke. This sets up the final situation as Sybil and Victor argue about Amanda and Elyot while Amanda and Elyot silently and ultimately conspiratorially observe them and form their bond again. Amanda and Elyot have no dialogue for the last

three pages of the play; their relationship is presented entirely
visually, counterpointed against the bickering of Victor and
Sybil. When Sybil slaps Victor and he shakes her as Amanda
and Elliot leave at the end of the play, it looks on the surface as
though Victor and Sybil have lost, and Amanda and Elyot have
won. That would be a limited reading, however, as throughout
the play we've been shown that human relationships are not
easy, that dangers lurk everywhere, and that romantic love
alone is not enough to sustain a relationship. Initially Victor
and Sybil stand for a rather passionless conventional existence
(the mythological Sybils were after all not only prophets but
also chaste old women) whereas Amanda and Elliot believe
in and live by a set of values where passion matters. They are
associated with energy and activity, whereas Sybil and Victor
are safe and stolid. In the first act, Amanda claims to have
seen Elyot running while he talks of her as the kind of natural
disaster, an earthquake or an exploding volcano. The social
rules cannot contain their vigour, but what they learn in the
course of the play is that for them to live life to the full involves
being prepared to suffer painfully, as well as to be ecstatically
happy. On the surface, it appears that they cannot live with one
another, but to live without one another is equally or even more
painful. Ultimately the play is therapeutic for the two other
characters as well as they move from their smugly conventional
stasis to a situation where real feelings are being expressed and
violent actions indulged in. The two leading characters arrive
at their understanding through trading insults, fighting and
saying that they hate one another, so it seems not unreasonable
to extend the same idea to their two spouses. The ending holds
out to Sybil and Victor the possibility of further growth: they
have moved away from their banal and conventional lives
into a whole new world of feeling. Perhaps the play does
show the triumph of incredibly selfish people, but since this
triumph of the self is extended to all the characters in the form
of extended self-knowledge which itself is the prerequisite for
further growth, it is not a purely selfish ending. We know that
Elyot and Amanda will continue to fight when their cosmic

thingummys don't gel, but also that their fighting is necessary if they are to live at all.

A Taste of Honey

Figure 7 A Taste of Honey *by Shelagh Delaney, directed by Bijan Sheibani. Kate O'Flynn (as Jo) and Eric Kofi Abrefa (as Jimmy). National Theatre, London, UK; February 2014. Credit: Nigel Norrington/ArenaPAL; www.arenapal.com*

Shelagh Delaney's *A Taste of Honey* (1958) has been lauded as an example of the ways in which various theatrical and social structures were attacked in the post-war world, particularly by a group of heterogeneous male writers who were lumped together as 'Angry Young Men'. Delaney herself claimed that her play was written quickly in response to a play by Terrence Rattigan that appeared to her to falsify many aspects of emotional experience. She modifies many Romantic Comedy scenarios to locate scenes of conventional courtship in an environment that is characterized by a working-class background, the absence of fathers and father figures, and the fecklessness of the heroine's mother. At times, the play appears to be on the verge of becoming a Romantic Comedy: Helen, the mother of the female protagonist Jo, is presented as being on the periphery of a marriage that teeters on the possibility of a happy ending, Jo could settle down with her sailor lover who promises marriage (Figure 7), the gay student who moves in with Jo could become her partner in nurturing her forthcoming baby, her mother might settle down to being a grandmother. However, the play offers these possibilities only to refute them. Moreover, the play also challenges stereotypes by making Jo's boyfriend (the father of her child) black and introducing a gay man who embodies many of the supporting maternal characteristics that Jo's own mother does not. Helen, her mother, is presented as, according to a stage direction, 'a semi-whore', with a knack of picking out as partners men who offer her no true sustenance. The play's setting is resolutely downbeat with a grotty flat surrounded by a slaughterhouse, a cemetery and a gasworks. The interior firmly locates the setting as at the lower end of the social scale: Jo makes minor attempts to soften the light by wrapping a scarf round a bare lightbulb but there is a bleakness to the set that is never fully ameliorated. Helen pursues a romantic vision that she will find a suitable partner and early scenes offer us two juxtaposed wooings as Jo and her boyfriend (who is effectively unnamed throughout the play, until the very end when he is referred to as Jimmy) play a romantic scenario in which he asks her to marry him while Helen and Peter, her lover, also negotiate their way to a wedding. The two contrasting narratives tend to undercut one another, and it is noteworthy that although the dialogue is elliptical and allusive rather than direct and open, Helen appears to have moved originally in order to escape from Peter who has managed to track her down anyway. Jo and the sailor plan to marry and Helen goes off to marry Peter, leaving Jo alone in the flat, where she spends the night with her boyfriend and, presumably, gets pregnant. In this play neither relationship actually works well: Jo is impregnated, and does not see the boy again, Helen finds herself in an abusive relationship that she will eventually leave. When we next see Jo, she is heavily pregnant and has a new male friend, Geoff, who is apparently gay, although some critics have taken some exception to Delaney's portrayal of the character which invests him with maternal characteristics and feminizes him as the caring figure that Helen never is.

The play is of its period and the eventual discovery that Jo's baby will be mixed race is a negative variant on the old romantic motif in which the forthcoming baby turns out to be the resolution of some long-standing communal difficulty, since Helen cannot stomach the idea of looking after a baby who will reveal her daughter's racial 'transgression'. Having thrown Geoff out and with him the prospect of an unusual but potentially nurturing child-rearing situation, Helen is not ready to take on the responsibility of looking after her grandchild and her exit leaves Jo alone unwittingly facing an unknown future. Some of the play's power derives not only from its economical presentation of the various scenarios but also from the fact that other romantic possibilities for happier endings are invoked subliminally through the underlying Romantic Comedy possibilities that it chooses to deny.

Stags and Hens

In Willy Russell's *Stags and Hens* (1978), separate groups of men (stags) and women (hens) have gathered to mark a prospective bride and groom's forthcoming marriage, but have accidentally found themselves at the same venue. With a large cast (twelve), that probably accounts for it not being staged often, *Stags and Hens* is set at a liminal moment sanctified by gendered responses to a forthcoming marriage in which friends of the prospective bride and groom separately celebrate the upcoming nuptials. The groups of men and women are sketched so that the women collectively appear to value marriage as an escape from the meaninglessness of their existence, while the men regard it as losing a friend and

giving in to powerful forces that will limit their lives. This is
not to say that the women take a romantic view of the married
state: Bernadette, the only one who is already married is asked
if she cried on the night before her wedding and replies: 'No
love. I've just been cryin' ever since!' (Russell 1996: 208). The
stags and hens try, both separately and together, to police the
relationship between Linda and Dave through their invocation
of and adherence to the rituals of the hen and stag nights, one of
the celebrations of forthcoming marriage, but they fail. On this
occasion, Linda, the potential bride, escapes her conventional
fate to run away with Peter, an ex-lover who has escaped the
town but is back to play a gig at the club. It is unclear whether
her decision will lead to a rekindled romantic relationship
with Peter, but it is clear that she has escaped a deadly status
quo. The key factor here is that she overcomes the forces of
patriarchy and escapes the limited vision of marriage that is on
offer. The play's characters present a vision of conformity and
stagnation as a response to the banality of their existence, but
the author plots Linda's way through the various constraints
of patriarchy and matrimony to refute the narrowing of
possibility that the stags and hens variously associate with the
wedding and with marriage. In this play marriage is a prison
and Linda's escape, in breaking the window of the Gents toilet
and taking up the offer of a lift in the group's van as they head
for Scotland, represents the quest for something better. Linda's
problem is that she feels as though she is getting married to
the whole town and everything it stands for: 'It's not just like
I'm marryin' Dave. It's like if I marry him I marry everythin'.
Like, I could sit down now an' draw you a chart of everythin'
that'll happen in my life after tomorrow' (Russell 1996:
216). The men associate marriage with a loss of freedom and
surrendering to the demands of family life, the women with
a form of minimal security in a hostile world. The fairy-tale
ending of Romantic Comedy is clearly not available to anyone
within the bounds of the play, but *Stags and Hens* remains
haunted by the tantalizing possibility that something better
than what is on offer might be available.

Beautiful Thing

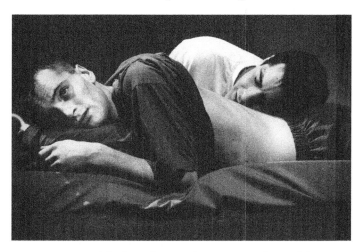

Figure 8 Beautiful Thing *by Jonathan Harvey, directed by Hettie Macdonald. Richard Dormer (as Ste) and Zubin Varla (as Jamie). Duke of York's Theatre, London, UK; September 1994. Credit: Henrietta Butler/ArenaPAL; www.arenapal.com*

Jonathan Harvey's *Beautiful Thing* (1993) relocates the whole action of the tentative beginnings of a love affair out of a traditional patriarchal context into what the play's subtitle calls an urban fairy-tale, which no doubt invokes the traditionally pejorative description of gay men as fairies. However, it also refers to the dreamy fairy-like quality of this tale of homosexual love awakening as the two male protagonists establish their romantic relationship in an apparently hostile environment (Figure 8), culminating in the kind of festive dance that traditionally celebrates a betrothal. This is even more marked in the 1996 film version which emphasizes the fairy-tale atmosphere as the population of a whole working-class estate joins in the final glitterball dance. Although the play opened at the tiny Bush Theatre in 1993 it enjoyed a successful West End run in 1994 and drew admiring reviews even from generally right-wing newspapers that might have been expected not to welcome its subject or its approach to it. One of the many interesting aspects of the presentation of the burgeoning love affair between the two adolescents, Ste and Jamie, is the fact that at the time the play was staged, the affair was actually illegal, since the (male) homosexual age of sexual consent was 21, whereas the heterosexual age of consent was 16. It was also a time of considerable debate about the effects of what was originally Clause 28 of the 1988 Local Government Bill that prevented local councils and schools from promoting the teaching of the acceptability of homosexuality as a pretended family relationship. This legal provision undoubtedly caused considerable hardship for many young people and it was only repealed in 2003. Although there is virtually no reference to this wider political environment in the play, the simple fact of showing an illegal relationship between two young men in a positive framework was daring. Few reviewers explicitly noted this, apart from Jeremy Kingston, reviewing the play's brief run at the Donmar Warehouse after it transferred from the Bush theatre, who criticized the politicians who had enacted a discriminatory age of consent for gay men and pointed out that 'beneath the unashamedly romantic schmaltz it's actually sanctioning criminal behaviour' (*What's On*: 13 April 1994), and Nicholas de Jongh who also swiped at the age of consent and the continuing malevolence of Section 28 in his description of the ending: 'the final tableau, with the two adolescent lovers dancing cheek-to-cheek in the sun, while Sandra and Leah follow suit is like a dream of homosexuals accepted in the family – instead of being rejected or outcast' (*Evening Standard*: 31 March 1994). The play ends as the young lovers and Leah and Sandra are about to set off on a voyage of discovery to a gay pub, beginning another quest in the search for acceptance.

The patriarchal forces we are shown are the traditional ones that operate within families, not in the wider world of politics: Ste's offstage father is a crude monster given to savage beatings of his younger son, while Jamie's mother Sandra and her ineffective boyfriend Tony are not shining examples of the virtues of heterosexual family relationships. The play begins with a potential heterosexual relationship being hinted at as Jamie and Leah, another sixteen-year-old, are cloud gazing. Leah is obsessed with Mama Cass of the pop group The Mamas and the Papas, ironically echoing the failings of the offstage mother and father in the play. When the play was first staged in 1993, she was played by the white actress Sophie Stanton but in the 1994 transfer the role was given to Diane Parish, who is black. None of the newspaper critics drew attention to the different racial appearance of the two actresses who played the role and there is nothing specific in the play to suggest that the character is either black or white.

The mutual relationship between the two boys soon develops via an extremely unsentimental scene in which Ste is given sanctuary for the night by Sandra when he is, routinely, beaten up by his drunkard father and brother. In her review of the Bush production Lynn Gardner welcomed 'an urban fairytale in which love really does change everything'. Gardner is sensitive to the underpinning details that create the mood: 'The boys' first tentative, tender sexual encounter takes place to the strains of You are 16 Going On 17 as Jamie's mother watches a re-run of the Sound of Music on Sky.' She suggests that '[i]t is as if the characters have all being touched by the generosity of love, which makes them the world through fresh eyes' as the 'fragile first love has a knock-on effect' on Sandra and Leah. She concludes:

A fantasy of course, and one which in less capable hands would have come across as sugary humbug, but Harvey crafts his play with astonishing maturity and grounds the drama in a tangible sense of reality. He draws his characters with such a delicate detail that when the fantasy takes flight the audience is more than ready for take off.

The cynical will argue that life just isn't like that. That Leah, Jamie and Ste are classic textbook 'victims' whose lives will end in unhappiness and unfulfilled dreams not a long, slow, comfortable snog in the warm sunshine to the sweet sound of the Mamas and the Papas.

But seldom has there been a play which so exquisitely and joyously depicts what it like to be 16, in the first flush of love and full of optimism. Truly a most unusual and beautiful thing.

(The Guardian: 2 August 1993)

The set itself is reminiscent of that for an ancient comedy with Sandra's flat as the central safe space guarded with greenery in the shape of a hanging basket and two flower tubs with another flat to either side, one containing the monstrous father, the other Leah and her equally offstage mother. When the play was restaged in the West End, Charles Spencer commented 'the play's best scene shows the two 16-year-olds sharing a bed together. The gaucheness, the rush of excitement and the inarticulate tenderness of young love are beautifully captured in writing of great truth and delicacy. Only the most irrational of homophobes could fail to be moved by it' (*Daily Telegraph*: 29 September 1994). John Gross wrote in the *Sunday Telegraph* 'I'm a sentimental soul, and I only wish people still wrote such sweet romantic confections about heterosexual lovers. (If they tried, I suspect they would be hooted off the stage.)' (2 October 1994).

East Is East

Ayub Khan-Din's *East Is East* (1996) dramatizes one of the traditional negative tropes of Romantic Comedy, showing the thwarting of a heavily patriarchal father's attempts to marry off his sons against their wishes. The situation is replete with complex class, race and gender issues: the patriarch George is of Pakistani origin, his wife Ella is white English, their seven children do not identify with Pakistani culture and the family runs a fish and chips shop. George brings Mr Shah, another patriarchal father of daughters, into the domestic environment to arrange marriages with two of his sons, but his attempt is thwarted in a farcical catastrophe and does not result in any kind of traditional romantic ending as, although his sons both escape arranged marriages, no-one marries a sweetheart. Khan-Din chose to set his semi-autobiographical play in 1971, twenty-five years before it first was staged, at a time of active fighting between India and Pakistan as well as growing racial tensions in the United Kingdom following the politician Enoch Powell's incendiary 1968 'Rivers of Blood' speech. George states that he came to England in 1930 (which means that either he is not technically a Pakistani or he somehow acquired his nationality at a later stage since Pakistan did not exist as a state until 1947), that he was an extra in a film in 1937 or 1938 (one of the Korda brothers' Indian films), and has a first wife in Pakistan who he has not seen for many years, but he has also had seven children with his white English wife Ella. George has a plan to marry off two of his sons, Abdul and Tariq, to the two daughters of Mr Shah, a rich butcher. Before the beginning of the play, Tariq, their eldest son has decamped from the family home to avoid an arranged marriage and has become a hairdresser (the 1999 film version opens out the action to include the hairdresser son, who appears to be camp if not necessarily an actual 'pansy' as his father describes him). Much of the action is taken up by delineations of the activities of the younger members of the family as they try to negotiate the everyday tribulations of being caught between two cultures. The play begins with the discovery that the twelve-year-old youngest son, Sajid, has somehow escaped being circumcised and culminates in the catastrophic and farcical moment when the sculpture of a vagina complete with pubic hair made by Saleem, an art student who his father believes is studying engineering, lands at the feet of Mr Shah. Both events are played as naturally occurring in the context of lived experience, but both access the territory of social conventions and rites of passage. Stir into the mix the fact that Ella's friend Annie is someone who prepares the bodies of the dead for burial and it is clear that another set of complex subtexts is running behind the naturalistic carapace.

Clearly this is not a typical Romantic Comedy since the action contrives to liberate two unwilling candidates from the arranged marriage that neither of them wants but does not take them as far as a union with another beloved. No rational case is made within the play for the possible benefits of arranged marriages and only George and Mr Shah of the onstage characters are in favour of the practice, even though George's possibly bigamous marriage to Ella was clearly not arranged. The sheer amount of violence within the play as George attacks Ella and also beats up Saleem militates against a simple view of its comedic elements, but I think that the overall picture is of a crisis of patriarchy and masculinity as George harkens back to a golden age of a rule-bound society in which the power of fathers was a given, rather than something that had to be earned. The Khan family is at the centre of a web of contradictions and conflicts that deftly represent the wider social fissures between integration and assimilation or standing by old traditions. David Nathan, writing in the *Jewish Chronicle* (29 November 1996), saw parallels between Jewish experience of exile and the situation of the Khans: '[T]he issue is not so much a culture clash, as the determination to impose a set of rules rooted in another world onto youngsters brought up in society which has repudiated traditional observances.' Simon Reade (*Time Out*: 27 November 1996) analysed the way the play worked thus: 'The playwright guides us beyond conventional responses to culture clashes and appalling wife-bashing, and delivers a hugely entertaining, highly involving, emotionally tender, politically inflamed family drama decrying the exploitation of race and women and children by men drilled by the puny patriarchy the world over.' The original staging, a co-production between Birmingham Rep, Tamasha and the Royal Court, was seen at various venues in London and subsequently there were co-productions between York Theatre Royal, Pilot Theatre and the Bolton Octagon in 2005, Birmingham Rep in 2009, and at the Trafalgar Studios in 2014 (with the author playing George) where Georgina Brown in the *Mail on Sunday* (26 October 2014) astutely drew attention to the romantic elements in the portrayal of George's relationship with Ella 'There's a suggestion that this marriage was a love match. He can still get round her with his Urdu love songs and tender shoulder massages.' Stage directions bear this out, drawing attention to the marital routines that suggest a shared

Figure 9 East Is East *by Ayub Khan-Din, from the 1999 film directed by Damien O'Donnell. Om Puri (as George) and Linda Bassett (as Ella). Credit: Marilyn Kingwill/ArenaPAL; www.arenapal.com*

intimacy in their banter: 'George grins slightly, these arguments happen all the time and this one has reached its point' (Khan-Din 1996: 6). Similarly Ella responds to his threat to bring over his first wife from Pakistan 'taking it in good humour' as she tells him to 'Piss off' (Khan-Din 1996: 7) (Figure 9). There is a great deal of humour at the expense of customs around eating and dressing with the children being forced to frantically hide the smell of their illicit bacon sandwiches from their father with wafts of curry powder and the only daughter Meenah being forced into a sari for the visit of Mr Shah only for it to be dismissed by him with the put down that 'You should wear Shalwar kameeze' (Khan-Din 1996: 54).

The play's setting, now some fifty years in the past, may help to defuse some of the unwelcome and outdated social attitudes of some of its characters and allow for a greater leeway in addressing the iniquities of the situation, but as Ella's friend Annie remarks perceptively the big battle may yet be to come when the lively only daughter Meenah reaches what George would think of as a marriageable age. The play's apparently relatively uncomplicated and comic view of the tensions between Islam and secular western society and also of the paternal and marital violence that erupts in the family from time to time might have led to it becoming more difficult to stage in the current climate. However, the general critical reactions to the 2021 National Theatre co-production with Birmingham Rep to celebrate the play's twenty-fifth anniversary suggest that it has escaped relatively unchallenged on such issues.

Khan-Din, like Tanika Gupta later, also engaged with another example of the English comedic tradition related to marriage, specifically the reality of what follows the wedding ceremony. In his case, he adapted Bill Naughton's *All in Good Time* (television 1961 as *Honeymoon Postponed*, staged 1963, filmed in 1966 as *The Family Way*) as *Rafta, Rafta* (itself filmed in 2011 under the title *All in Good Time*) in which a newly married couple are unable to consummate their marriage on their first night together in the face of familial pressures and subsequently the difficulties of their housing situation (living with family) which mean they are never in a relaxed enough situation to contemplate consummation.

Meet the Mukherjees

Tanika Gupta's *Meet the Mukherjees* (2008) is an example of a play that deliberately tackles the issues of racial prejudice between different ethnic minorities head on, using the matrix of Romantic Comedy to open up some very sensitive subjects. As in Khan-Din's *East Is East*, the play uses a cast of actors from ethnic minorities to populate the stage. In this case, in the production at Bolton in 2008, the heroine Anita's best friend was played by the only white actor in the cast, as an outsider to the two dominant groups within the play, the West Indians and the East African Asians. The premise is simple enough: Anita, daughter of East African Asian parents, starts a relationship with Aaron, son of West Indian parents, as revenge on her mother Chitra for her worrying about Anita being left on the shelf. Much to Anita's surprise, the relationship becomes serious, and they have to confront many obstacles to arrive at an agreement to marry. The climactic moment that concludes the first act is when Chitra, on a surprise visit to Anita's flat discovers a naked Aaron hiding from her in Anita's wardrobe. Chitra, anxious about Anita's status has already recalled her dead husband Montu from paradise to advise her how to tackle the situation and also summoned his brother Raj (doubled with Montu in production) to head the family response. Neither of the mothers welcomes the possibility of a formal relationship with the other family and there is a brisk rehearsal of prejudices and stereotypes about other ethnic groups on all sides that excoriates, amongst others, black baby fathers, the English, Bengalis, arranged marriages, lesbians, family honour, Hindus, Muslims, Christians, Indians, West Indians, Gujaratis, Australians, Jews, Punjabis, Sikhs,

South Indians, Marwaris and Sri Lankans. Uncle Raj voices many of these prejudices and is effectively judged by fact that Anita leaves him alone to continue his diatribe while she goes offstage to the toilet, returning while he is still in full flow. In the confrontation between the families, Anita learns that Aaron has a teenaged daughter (India) and, feeling betrayed that he has acted so stereotypically and failed to tell her, she breaks off the relationship. Aaron attempts a reconciliation by arriving outside her flat to put his case in a dialogue that focuses on the problems they face:

> **Anita:** Please Aaron – let's just call it a day. I can't handle this. It's bad enough with you and me being different.
> **Aaron:** What d'you mean 'different'?
> **Anita:** Asians and Afro-Caribbeans don't have a great history of getting on. You said as much.
> **Aaron:** We can change it.
> **Anita:** Yeah right.
> **Aaron:** It shouldn't matter.
> **Anita:** But it does.
>
> (Gupta 2008: 101)

After he goes down on one knee to ask her to marry him, Aaron eventually climbs up to her balcony in a scene that owes more than a little to *Romeo and Juliet* and then punctuates their dialogue with seductive kisses. Negotiating their ways through the challenges and expectations of the two families in respect of marriage ceremonies, the protagonists eventually challenge the normative voices of both mothers and the last we see of them is both mothers eying each other up 'warily' and 'reluctantly' raising their glasses in a 'tense celebration' (Gupta 2008: 119). The final scene speaks to a happy ending as Chitra hosts Aaron's child India on her way back from school, dropping in for Bollywood movies and samosas, while Montu, who has to return to paradise, ends the story with all the omniscient authority of a Victorian novel, prophesying that they will all live happily ever after.

Beginning

Figure 10 Beginning *by David Eldridge, directed by Polly Findlay. Justine Mitchell (as Laura); Sam Troughton (as Danny). Ambassador's Theatre, London, UK; 13 January 2018. Credit: Manuel Harlan/ ArenaPAL; www.arenapal.com*

Romantic Comedies traditionally end with at least one wedding and, by implication at least, a couple (or couples) living 'happily ever after'. Sometimes as in the final blessing of *A Midsummer Night's Dream*, in the proviso scene of *The Way of the World* or at the end of *Meet the Mukherjees*, the action also adumbrates the fates of the eventual children that will be the product of those marriages. In David Eldridge's two-hander *Beginning* (2017) the crux of the play is whether or not Danny, the male protagonist, will have unprotected sex with the ovulating heroine Laura. Many issues that could only have been hinted at allusively in previous comedies are tackled explicitly here as the characters spar over not only whether they will have sex but also whether it should carry the possibility of procreation.

The surrounding cast who might have had an impact on the decision in other plays have vanished and the conventions and inhibitions of courtship are scrutinized in what is essentially an elongated proviso scene, as the couple negotiate the conditions that will govern their prospective congress. Procrastination and subterfuge become the main obstacles to consummation, as Danny tries to compute the issues that could arise from him impregnating Laura (Figure 10). This is an interesting example of Cavell's comedy of remarriage, since not only has Danny been married before, but he also has a daughter, a rare example of a protagonist's offspring being mentioned in Romantic Comedy. Another significant factor related to this is that the couple are not young. As Dominic Maxwell wrote in *The Times* (13 October 2017): 'This is rom-com as it ought to be, in which the obstacles to not-as-young-as they-used to[-]be love are rooted in real, human truths: some gnarly, some matter-of-fact – all rendered with a wondrous wit that never extends into caricature.'

The play occurs in real time and the dialogue ranges widely over many of the contexts of contemporary romantic attachments and the patriarchal issues that can arise in negotiating a firm basis for a sexual encounter. Danny's many procrastinating subterfuges include a commitment to preparing the ground for the potential sexual encounter by clearing up after Laura's house-warming party, including a moment when he asks for the Marigolds, protective gloves for use in domestic cleaning, that operate as a potential metaphor for the condoms that may or may not be used in an eventual sexual encounter. The rules of engagement in the fantasies the protagonists anticipate for the morning after mean that the single available condom need not be used in the imminent sexual encounter since they imagine that they may have sex again in the morning, but Danny's eventually makes a decision and 'places the condom gently to one side' (Eldridge 2018: 80), which suggests that they are about to begin a process with an unknown but potentially positive outcome. It is not a wedding, but the situation is fraught with the possibilities of the commitment that typifies Romantic Comedy.

'No epilogue, I pray you' (Shakespeare [1600] 2017: 5.1.346)

This book is not a history of Romantic Comedy nor even a history of English Romantic Comedy. I have selected a range of plays for discussion that explore many different aspects of what a Romantic Comedy might be at different times and in various places and tried to locate them in their appropriate contexts, drawing on historical and cultural material that may explain some of their particular features.

There can be no definitive conclusion because the genre is alive and well and one that is likely to be playing soon at a theatre near you. Romantic Comedy insists on the virtues of life and the joys of finding a place for a couple who truly value one another in building a society that is happier and healthier than the one envisaged by those who oppose them. Sometimes it has interpreted the betrothal or the marriage ceremony as a shorthand for living 'happily ever after' but in doing so it has spoken to a benevolent fantasy that we can achieve a wholeness and a completeness that defies time and safeguards the future of humankind.

The genre is characterized by a generosity towards its antagonists and expends a great deal of energy in trying to keep them within the comic synthesis, but it also recognizes that this may not be easy and may not even be possible. In recent years, it has been refreshed by a willingness to move outside its traditional boundaries to look again at issues of class, race and gender that demand to be addressed within modern society in ways that will sustain and nurture individuals who have not always been considered as suitable to be the subjects of sustained consideration within Romantic Comedy.

NOTES

Introduction

1 Hirst (1979) remains the best introduction to the genre.

2 The following works contain substantial discussions of the nature of comedy that illuminate my discussion of Romantic Comedy: Palmer (ed.) (1984), Segal (2001), Lowe (2007), Romanska and Ackerman (eds) (2017), Bowring (2019), Díez and Iacona (2021).

3 I have found the following studies are very useful in helping me to understand the subtleties of Roman and Greek theatre practice: Sandbach (1977), Hunter (1985), McLeish and Griffiths (2003), Marshall (2006), Revermann (ed.) (2014), Revermann (ed.) (2017).

4 Omitowoju (2002), Deacy and Pierce (eds) (2012), Akrigg and Tordoff (eds) (2013).

5 Wiles (1991), Traill (2008).

6 McLeish (1991), Dintner (ed.) (2019).

7 Dusinberre (1975), Martindale and Taylor (eds) (2004).

8 For important studies see Propp [1958] (2015), Bakhtin (1968), Bettelheim (1976), Krueger (ed.) (2000), Chaffee and Crick (2015).

9 See the introductions in Fitzsimmons and Gardner (eds) (1991) and Chotia (ed.) (1998).

10 There are trenchant examinations of the realities of courtship and marriage in England in Shorter (1976), Stone (1977), Stone (1990), Porter and Hall (1995), Dabhoiwala (2012), Dyhouse (2021).

11 Sinfield (1999).

Chapter 1

1   These dates are taken from Taylor and Loughnan (2017: 484–5).
2   See Bakhtin (1968) and Bristol (1985).

Chapter 2

1   For an exploration of her work, see Burkert (2021).

REFERENCES

Akrigg, Ben and Rob Tordoff, eds (2013), *Slaves and Slavery in Ancient Greek Comic Drama*, Cambridge: Cambridge UP.

Bakhtin, Mikhail (1968), *Rabelais and His World*, Bloomington, IN: Indiana UP.

Bettelheim, Bruno (1976), *The Uses of Enchantment*, London: Thames & Hudson.

Book of Common Prayer, The (1662), https://www.churchofengland.org/prayer-and-worship/worship-texts-and-resources/book-common-prayer (accessed 17 May 2021).

Boucicault, Dion ([1840] 2010), *London Assurance*, ed. Trevor R. Griffiths, London: Nick Hern Books.

Bowring, Finn (2019), *Erotic Love in Sociology, Philosophy and Literature*, London: Bloomsbury Academic.

Brighouse, Harold (n.d.), *Hobson's Choice*, London: Samuel French.

Bristol, Michael D. (1985), *Carnival and Theater: Plebeian Culture and the Structure of Authority in Renaissance England*, London: Methuen.

Burkert, Mattie (2021), *Speculative Enterprise: Public Theaters and Financial Markets in London, 1688–1763*, Charlottesville, VA: U of Virginia P.

Cavell, Stanley (1981), *Pursuits of Happiness: the Hollywood Comedy of Remarriage*, Cambridge, MA: Harvard UP.

Centlivre, Susanna ([1718] 1969), *A Bold Stroke for a Wife*, ed. Thalia Stathas, London: Arnold.

Centlivre, Susanna ([1718] 1995), *A Bold Stroke for a Wife*, ed. Nancy Copeland, Peterborough, ON: Broadview.

Chaffee, Judith and Olly Crick, eds (2015), *The Routledge Companion to Commedia dell' Arte*, London: Routledge.

Chotia, Jean, ed. (1998), *The New Woman and Other Emancipated Women Plays*, Oxford: Oxford UP.

Coleridge, Samuel Taylor ([1818] 1897), *Lectures and Notes on Shakespeare and Other English Poets*, ed. T. Ashe, London: George Bell and Sons.

Coward, Noël ([1930] 2000), *Private Lives*, London: Methuen.

Coward, Noël (1934), *Private Lives*, in *Play Parade*, London: Heinemann.

Dabhoiwala, Faramerz (2012), *The Origins of Sex*, London: Allen Lane.

Deacy, Susan and Karen F. Pierce, eds (2012), *Rape in Antiquity: Sexual Violence in the Greek and Roman Worlds*, London: Bristol Classical Press (Bloomsbury).

Delaney, Shelagh (1959), *A Taste of Honey*, London: Methuen.

Díez José, A. and Andrea Iacona (2021), *A Short Philosophical Guide to the Fallacies of Love*, London: Bloomsbury.

Dintner Martin, T., ed. (2019), *The Cambridge Companion to Roman Comedy*, Cambridge: Cambridge UP.

Dusinberre, Juliet (1975), *Shakespeare and the Nature of Women*, London: Macmillan.

Dyhouse, Carol (2021), *Love Lives*, Oxford: Oxford UP.

Elam, Keir (2002), *The Semiotics of Theatre and Drama*, 2nd ed., London: Routledge.

Eldridge, David (2018), *Beginning*, London: Methuen.

Fitzsimmons, Linda and Viv Gardner, eds (1991), *New Woman Plays*, London: Methuen.

Frye, Northrop ([1957] 1990), *Anatomy of Criticism*, Princeton, NJ: Princeton UP, London: Penguin.

Gardner, Viv and Susan Rutherford, eds (1992), *The New Woman and Her Sisters: Feminism and Theatre 1850–1914*, Hemel Hempstead: Harvester Wheatsheaf.

Goldsmith, Oliver ([1773] 1999), *She Stoops to Conquer*, ed. Trevor R. Griffiths, London: Nick Hern Books.

Griffiths, Trevor R., ed. (1996), *A Midsummer Night's Dream*: *Shakespeare in Production*, Cambridge: Cambridge UP.

Griffiths, Trevor R. and Simon Trussler, eds (2005), *Restoration Comedy*, London: Nick Hern Books.

Gupta, Tanika (2019), *Hobson's Choice*, adapted from *Hobson's Choice* by Harold Brighouse, London: Oberon Books.

Gupta, Tanika (2008), *Meet the Mukherjees*, London: Oberon Books.

Harvey, Jonathan (1994), *Beautiful Thing*, London: Methuen.

Hirst, D. L. (1979), *Comedy of Manners*, London: Methuen.

Houghton, Stanley ([1912] 2012), *Hindle Wakes*, London: Sidgwick and Jackson, Oberon.

Hume, Robert D. (1977), 'Marital Discord in English Comedy from Dryden to Fielding', *Modern Philology*, vol. 74, no. 3: 248–72. *JSTOR*, www.jstor.org/stable/437114 (accessed 22 April 2021).

Hunter, R. L. (1985), *The New Comedy of Greece and Rome*, Cambridge: Cambridge UP.

Khan-Din, Ayub (1996), *East Is East*. London: Nick Hern Books.

Krueger Roberta, L., ed. (2000), *The Cambridge Companion to Medieval Romance*, Cambridge: Cambridge UP.

Leach, Edmund (1973), 'Structuralism in Social Anthropology', in David Robey (ed.), *Structuralism*, 37–56, Oxford: Oxford UP.

Lowe, N. J. (2007), *Comedy*, Cambridge: Cambridge UP.

Marshall, C. W. (2006), *The Stagecraft and Performance of Roman Comedy*, Cambridge: Cambridge UP.

Martindale, Charles and A. B. Taylor, eds (2004) *Shakespeare and the Classics*, Cambridge: Cambridge UP.

McLeish, Kenneth (1991), *Roman Comedy*, Bristol: Bristol Classical Press.

McLeish, Kenneth and Trevor R. Griffiths (2003), *Guide to Greek Theatre and Drama*, London: Bloomsbury.

Menander (1994), *Aristophanes and Menander New Comedy*, ed., trans. and intro. Kenneth McLeish and J. Michael Walton, London: Methuen.

Omitowoju, Rosanna (2002), *Rape and the Politics of Consent in Classical Athens*, Cambridge: Cambridge UP.

Palmer, D. J., ed. (1984), *Comedy: Developments in Criticism*, London: Macmillan.

Pettet, E. C. ([1949] 1970), *Shakespeare and the Romance Tradition*, London: Methuen.

Porter, Roy and Lesley Hall (1995), *The Facts of Life: The Creation of Sexual Knowledge in Britain, 1650–1950*, New Haven, CT: Yale UP.

Propp, Vladimir ([1958] 2015), *Morphology of the Folk Tale*, Mansfield Centre, CT: Martino Publishing.

Revermann, Martin, ed. (2014), *The Cambridge Companion to Greek Comedy*, Cambridge: Cambridge UP.

Revermann, Martin, ed. (2017), *A Cultural History of Theatre in Antiquity*, London: Bloomsbury.

Romanska, Magda and Alan Ackerman, eds (2017), *Reader in Comedy*, London: Methuen Drama.

Russell, Willy (1996), *Stags and Hens in Russell Plays: 1*, London: Methuen Drama.

Sandbach, H. (1977), *The Comic Theatre of Greece and Rome*, London: Chatto & Windus.

Segal, Erich (2001), *The Death of Comedy*, Cambridge, MA: Harvard UP.

Shakespeare, William ([1600] 1964), *Much Ado about Nothing*, ed. David L Stevenson, New York: Signet.

Shakespeare, William ([1600] 2017), *A Midsummer Night's Dream*, ed. Sukanta Chaudhuri, Arden Shakespeare 3rd series, London: Bloomsbury.

Shakespeare, William ([1623] 2008), *Twelfth Night*, ed. Keir Elam, London: Arden Shakespeare 3rd series, London: Bloomsbury.

Shorter, Edward (1976), *The Making of the Modern Family*, London: Collins.

Sinfield, Alan (1999), *Out on Stage: Lesbian and Gay Theatre in the Twentieth Century*, New Haven, CT: Yale UP.

Stone, Lawrence (1977), *The Family, Sex and Marriage in England 1500–1800*, London: Weidenfeld & Nicholson.

Stone, Lawrence (1990), *Road to Divorce: England 1530–1987*, Oxford: Oxford UP.

Taylor, Gary and Rory Loughnan (2017), 'The Canon and Chronology of Shakespeare's Works', in Gary Taylor and Gabriel Egan (eds), *The New Oxford Shakespeare Authorship Companion*, 417–602, Oxford: Oxford UP.

Traill, Ariana (2008), *Women and the Comic Plot in Menander*, Cambridge: Cambridge UP.

Tuveson, Ernest (1953), 'The Importance of Shaftesbury', *ELH*, vol. 20, no. 4: 267–99. *JSTOR*, www.jstor.org/stable/2871968 (accessed 28 April 2021).

Wiles, David (1991), *The Masks of Menander*, Cambridge: Cambridge UP.

INDEX

Characters from plays are cited with given names first (e.g. Obadiah Prim) followed by an abbreviated title (e.g. *Stroke*)

Printed in Great Britain
by Amazon

28082847R00106